Springtime Christmas Town

Springtime Christmas Town

Kathy Elaine Ribble

TATE PUBLISHING
AND ENTERPRISES, LLC

Published by Tate Publishing & Enterprises, LLC
127 E. Trade Center Terrace | Mustang, Oklahoma 73064 USA
1.888.361.9473 | www.tatepublishing.com

Tate Publishing is committed to excellence in the publishing industry. The company reflects the philosophy established by the founders, based on Psalm 68:11,
"The Lord gave the word and great was the company of those who published it."

Book design copyright © 2014 by Tate Publishing, LLC. All rights reserved.
Cover design by Joseph Emnace
Interior design by Joana Quilantang

Published in the United States of America

ISBN: 978-1-62994-284-1
1. Fiction / Romance / General
2. Fiction / General
14.01.15

Dedication

I want to thank the Lord Jesus Christ for my salvation and everything he has done in my life.

To my wonderful husband, who has always believed in me and is the love of my life,

To my best friend Charmayne, who I can call day or night with any prayer request,

To my mother, who has always been there for me,

To my children, Kim, Dave, Eric, and Hope,

To my grandchildren Aaron, MaKayla, Ryan, and Jace

To my sister Janis, I love you.

Contents

Kerri's Reflection

As Kerri walked through the door of her newly decorated townhome, she smiled as she looked around; she was very pleased with the result of all her hard work. When she had first looked at the property, she really liked the layout and the location, but the way it had been decorated was so cold; Kerri knew she could warm the place up with just the right colors and furniture. Kerri bought the townhome after she had moved back to Christmas Town and dealt with her parent's estate. Tom and Deanne Johnson were wonderful people and everyone who knew them loved them. Kerri could not understand how two wonderful people as her parents could die so suddenly and tragically as they did. Kerri's parents were coming home from a Holy Land trip to Isreal. As far back as she could remember, they had talked about going to the Holy Land, and walking where Jesus walked.

Kerri never really understood why they had such a desire to go, but she wanted them to be happy, so when she graduated college and gotten her first job, she made it a priority to put money aside to a savings account, and saved for the money to buy two trips to the Holy Land with one of they're favorite ministers, which included round trip tickets, hotel and meals for seven days. Kerri surprised her parents with the trip on their twenty-fifth anniversary, oh, how many times she wished she had never given them that trip, even though many people tried to console her, and told her they were really happy now, and were with the Father in heaven, and God always has reasons for allowing things to happen that we don't and can't understand sometimes, but to be grateful that she got to be part of their dream, and the fact that God had used her in helping them to achieve their dream.

Oh, but how she missed those two wonderful people; they were such great parents. She had heard her friends complain about their parents; she just could not relate to how they did not get along with their parents because she and her mother had always been close and her father had always been the life of every party; he had such a wonderful personality and was always joking around. Kerri never went a whole week without having a long conversation with one of them. Tom and Deanne Johnson were very loved, they had many friends and were always willing to help everyone and anyone in need. It was really no surprise that their memorial service was standing room only because people who knew and loved them packed the place out. Everyone had genuine concern for her, they all knew how much her parents had meant to her, and how much she had meant to her parents.

Many of her parents' friends knew how concerned her parent's had been about her future, some of whom she had known all of her life and some new friends of her parents she had just met since moving back to Christmas Town. Kerri did not have any idea that her parents had asked them to pray for her, and as she found out later, they didn't just say they would pray, they would get down on their knees and pray until they had peace, or have the answer to their prayers manifest, in fact that was where she had been that morning, to the church she grew up in, her father had been a deacon, and her mother a Sunday school teacher; they were always willing to work anywhere they were needed. Kerri didn't think her parents ever missed a church service, or an event held at the church, at least that she knew of, unless it was unavoidable or due to an illness.

As far as she could remember growing up, she thought she was at the church as much as she was at home, at least until she went off to college; and then she was so busy, she couldn't get home to go to church with her parents, though she had tried a couple of churches while going to college, they didn't feel right and were actually downright boring when she really thought about it. The memorial service had been even harder because her parents had died in a plane crash coming home from Israel, and because she still felt so much guilt for sending them on the trip. Even though everyone told her they knew they were very excited to have gotten to go, and most people would never have the chance to get to do something they dreamed of all of their lives, and now her parents were happy in heaven. Kerri wished she could go back in time, and change everything she possibly could to not have given them the trip, to have gone to church with them the last time they asked her. Kerri's parents had tried to talk to her about her spiritual life, and she would change the subject, avoid the topic as much as possible, or just ignore them altogether. They were very concerned about her not being involved in church, the way she was when she was growing up. The truth was she wasn't able to get into church the way she used to, she knew she had fallen away from the Lord.

She would try to pray and would get distracted by something, or someone she would try to read the Word, but would get distracted from that also. Before Kerri had left for college, she had allowed some things that happened to her at the church to leave her hurt and bitter, so she hadn't been able to find peace because she couldn't seem to forgive in this particular situation, and she knew she needed to forgive, but hadn't been able to get to that place in her life. Then she got the call about her parents' plane crash, and it took all of her effort to deal with the death of her parents. After the memorial service, Kerri resigned from the mortgage company she had been working at since graduating college, she had moved back to Christmas Town, and settled her parents estate and sold the home where she had grown up and bought the townhome. She didn't regret selling the old home; she just wanted to get a fresh start. Kerri had found her townhome close to the bank, where she had gotten a job in their loan department. She looked around the house; she had just finished the remodeling and the decorating, she was pleased with the result.

After leaving church, she went by the Chinese restaurant to pick up some take-out of kung pao chicken and an egg roll, she then went home to order a movie while eating take-out, then took a nap on the perfect afternoon.

Brad's Introspection

Brad always started his day with praying and reading the Word of God; he knew without the Lord's help, he would not trust any decisions he made because he didn't make any decision without the Lord's help; he had submitted total control of his life to the Lord. When he finished praying, he looked out the window and realized it had started raining. As he was looking out the window, he was glad he had made the decision to come to this town; it had taken a lot of prayer and soul searching; he had also done a lot of research on the town.

Brad had been an architect for about four years and had worked for a big firm in the southwest, and had been offered a senior position in the company with a very impressive salary. Most people would think he was crazy to turn down such an opportunity and strike out on his own. Brad was a pioneer and a strong believer in the Lord, who guided him in every decision of his life. While he was in college, the young people he went to school with thought he was a little strange at first, until they had been around him for a while and then they all came to respect him. Brad even had an opportunity to help some of them.

When Brad made the decision to move to Christmas Town and told his parents, they were a little bit taken aback at first, but they knew they had raised their son right and knew he would not make that kind of decision unless he was sure, and even though they would miss him, they knew they had to let him go even though they had heavy hearts; they knew what God wanted was best; they prayed for him and blessed him, and they knew he would go forth with much faith and determination so, John and Mary Kensington bid their son good–bye. They had brought there son up to think for himself, and finish strong on anything he started.

John, Brad's father, had offered Brad the money to help him get started in his new venture, but Brad wanted to stand on his own two feet; he had saved some money, but knew he would need a small business loan to help him make it through his first year, just until he could get established as an architect in the area. While doing his research on the area, he found this was a very good area for growth, and that there was a lot of expansion and renovation planned for the area.

Brad looked at his watch and realized it was getting late; he had much to do, he had to set up appointments for the business phones and internet to be installed.

17

Brad had to set up a loan interview at the bank, and he still had to find just the right desk and drawing table. Brad realized it was getting chilly in the room, and he thought he had better check out the furnace and make sure it was working right. The building he had rented was going to serve not only as his business, but his apartment as well. The landlord was a very nice man he had met on his first trip to Christmas Town by the name of Bill Love, and they hit it off right away. In fact Bill had invited Brad to come to his church, so Brad had gone to Bill's church and found his church home in Christmas Town. Bill had told Brad, he did not care what he did with or to the building, he wanted Brad to have free reign because Bill had sized Brad up and felt he could trust Brad, and thought the young man had a very good future. Brad's first appointment was for the internet and phones to be connected, then he was supposed to meet with Bill and his new pastor Ted Jackson for lunch to discuss a gym that Brad had offered his services on to design because Brad loved to give any way he could. The three men decided to go ahead and start the process of designing the gym because the youth needed a place to meet and to stay out of trouble, but they wanted to design the gym is such a way that it could not only serve the youth, but also wedding receptions, overflow for extra people as they grew as a church, banquets, and dinners. The church had been growing rapidly the last year. After Brad had the luncheon meeting with Bill and Pastor Ted, he had to go by the bank to meet with the loan officer, and get the paper work started for the loan. Brad did not really know how much to ask for, but he knew the Lord would tell him before he had to answer that question, he knew the loan officer would ask him, but so far that question he had asked the Lord had went unanswered, oh well he knew when the right time came, he would have his answer. Brad realized he might need a jacket since a cold front was suppose to hit in, and it sure was beginning to feel that way, so he decided he needed to find the box that he had stored his winter jackets in, and when he reached in and pulled his jacket out of the box, something fell to the floor and he realized it was a picture he had not looked at in a long time. Brad knew he had not packed the picture, his mother must have put it in the box the day she had come to help him pack. Well he didn't have time to chase those rabbits, he would have to deal with that later.

The Meeting

Kerri had gotten to the office early Monday morning, put the coffee on, and was going through her messages when the phone rang; it was Gina her secretary telling Keri she was going to be late to work, which lately was fairly normal for Gina. Gina was a wonderful secretary and she could not ask for anyone better at her job than Gina was Or with a better fitting personality to work with her personality because they really worked well together, but lately Gina had been coming in late and had been very distracted, and Kerri knew something was going on with Gina, and knew she was going to have to have a talk with her sooner than later before the office started to suffer. Well that was something else to add to her list for the week; at some point, she had to take time to have a serious talk with Gina. Well she had better get busy, she had several loans to go over and put last minute notes on for Gina to make few phones calls and update the files.

Kerri submitted several loans the week before, and had to make appointments to let the applicants know where they stood with their loans. Kerri looked up as Gina walked through the door, and Kerri held up her hand and said, "Hold on Gina I don't want any explanations right now; however, sometime in the near future, preferably this week, we need to sit down and have a talk, but right now we need to get to work," Gina nodded her head and went to her desk and started to work. Kerri was so engrossed in her work she was.

Startled when Gina knocked on her door, and Kerri looked up, and Gina was grinning like someone who had just won the lottery, she said your three o'clock is here, and Kerri said, no way, it can't be three o'clock yet, and Gina said oh, but it is. Kerri asked Gina why she looked like the cat that swallowed the canary. Gina said oh I just met someone very interesting, and I believe you will find your next appointment let's just say a nice change of pace. Kerri just looked at Gina with vague curiosity thinking, *oh no I have some nut out there,* and went about bracing herself for the inevitable; oh, she had had nuts in her office before. Once she had had a man in her office who said he should be trusted because he was related to the president of the United States, and loan him some money, she had almost had to call the police to get rid of him, but she finally got him to understand that was not the way the banking industry worked; the security guards did come and escort him out, and later they learned that the man had a nervous breakdown, and he had escaped from the hospital and his sister had accidentally left his room door open, and he came to the bank as a walk-in. Since then, Kerri did not want to take walk-ins. Oh well couldn't be helped, once in a while a nut will even get by the screening process. Kerri nodded to Gina and said, "You can send them, him, or her in." Gina said it's a *he*, and what a *he*, wow. Well, Gina got a silly grin on her face, Kerry gave her a look that said, "Wipe off that silly grin on your face, or he will think your addle minded."

"Ok, don't say I didn't warn you." Gina left the office and sent him in.

"Now, I wonder what that girl was talking about. If it was some kind of nut, Gina would have warned me." A few minutes later, Gina came in and said, "May I introduce Mr. Brad Kensington, and Mr. Kensington this is Kerri Johnston, President of our Loan Department."

Kerri knew she was staring right through the young man she had been introduced to. She held out her hand to shake the young man's hand, and when she did, she felt something strange happen to her; she felt her insides start jumping up and down and making her feel giddy and funny all at the same time. Kerri heard herself say, "Hello Mr. Kensington may I help you?" While looking into the most beautiful blue eyes she had ever seen, and he had to be more than six foot tall with broad shoulders and beautiful dark wavy hair and looked as if he had just came in from the sun; his skin was a golden tan, and if that wasn't enough, he had the most beautiful smile she had ever seen. Kerri said to herself, *girl you need to get a grip on yourself before this man thinks you're the one that is addle minded.*

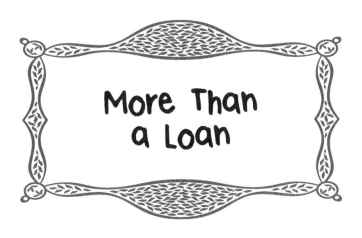

More Than a Loan

Brad had enjoyed the luncheon with his friend Bill and his new pastor, Pastor Ted Jackson. Brad felt they had accomplished quite a bit by the end of the lunch; he felt they all knew what was needed and what they wanted to do. They decided to have Brad go ahead and draw up some preliminary blue prints, and then meet again to go over everything. Brad wanted to have the guys over and cook for them since he was also an amateur chef and enjoyed cooking, and by then his office would be ready and they could lay out the blue prints in his office. Brad told Bill and Pastor Ted that he had a meeting at the Liberty National Bank at three o'clock and had to leave the meeting at two-thirty.

As Brad was leaving, Pastor Ted said, "I am not trying to intrude or be nosy, but if you don't mind my asking, who is your meeting with?" Brad said he didn't have a name, just the department. Pastor Ted said he was just curious because he had a friend whose parents had been killed in a plane crash; she moved back to Christmas Town after her parents' death, and he hadn't had a chance to visit her since she had moved back, but had heard she went to work in an executive position at Liberty National. Brad thought, *How awful.* Pastor Ted said the last time he had seen the girl was at her parents' memorial, and said she was very angry at the Lord at the time, and that he had known her parents very well and knew that they would not be pleased if they knew she was mad and angry at the Lord for what happened to them.

Pastor Ted said that he had tried to speak with her at the memorial, but didn't think she heard a word he said, and didn't think she was ready to listen. Pastor Ted said there was more to the young woman's story than he could actually share, but that the young woman needed lots of prayer. Brad took in all that Pastor Ted had said and filed it away in the back of his mind. Afterwards, he realized he hadn't ask Pastor Ted her name. Brad arrived at the bank just before three o'clock, and gave the secretary his card, and said he was there for a three o'clock appointment with the loan department. Brad had a seat to wait until he was called and led into an office. In his mind, he started going over everything he had done that day, he knew he was getting closer to having his business up and running. Brad was getting very excited, and was making a mental note to ask around about where to go to buy a desk, drafting table, filing cabinets, etc. When he happened to look up, he was startled to see the young lady who had been behind the desk standing in front of him, grinning from ear to ear and waiting on him to acknowledge her.

She introduced herself, "Hello, I am Gina" and reached out to shake his hand and he then introduced himself to her and followed her into the office. Brad almost laughed out loud when he heard her introduction of him to her boss, oh it was a normal introduction, but the way it was said was so dramatic that he thought to himself, he felt he was being presented to royal court. Brad thought this girl must be a hoot at a party, and the he looked away from Gina to the person he was being introduced to. That was when Brad froze in his tracks; no matter how hard he tried, he couldn't move his feet, or say anything at that particular moment because he was looking at a vision that looked like an angel with the afternoon sun shinning through the sheer panels that was over the window that made her look as if a glowing halo surrounded her.

Brad thought that she was one of the most beautiful women he had ever seen, she was about five-four, long-shiny-curly dark hair, huge blue eyes, and porcelain skin almost doll-like. Brad could not help himself the way he was looking at her, and he was so caught up in his own thoughts, he did not realize he was having the same effect on her. Gina always joking was even becoming uncomfortable and so she said, "Well, I will leave you to Miss Johnston."

Brad came to himself and said, "Nice to meet you," and then Kerri replied, "Nice to meet you also, please have a seat Mr. Kensington."

Brad said, "Please call me Brad."

"And please call me Kerri. Now, how can I help you, Mr. Kensington?"

Brad went in to explaining what he needed. Kerri listened to everything, then she opened a file cabinet and pulled out a package that was as thick as a book, and gave it to Brad and told him to please read the papers that was in the package and fill out the application, after which, that's the time they would decide which type of loan would be best for his purpose, then she asked him for a check for seventy-five dollars, so she could go ahead and get the credit report ordered.

She made another appointment with him for the next Thursday at the same time. When Brad left, he thought to himself how surreal that was, what a strange experience; he didn't know what to think; he had never had anything like that happen to him before, and didn't know what had just happened to him; he didn't know why Kerri had affected him the way she had. He had met beautiful women before and he had never felt like that before. Brad thought he would like to spend some time with her and get to know her, but he knew that was a dangerous train of thought. Brad had been through a lot and he did not want to get involved with anyone too fast. Brad knew what he had to do; he had to go and pray. There was one thing Brad knew, and that is God put people into his life for a reason, and he knew down deep in his soul that Kerri was going to be in his life, he just didn't know in what aspect yet, but he knew the Father would let him know what to do, so he had to get home and pray for a while.

Over Coffee

Kerri was finishing up her day; what an odd day it was too. Kerri was sitting at her desk going over the last of her work when she started thinking about her day and meeting Brad Kensington. He sure seemed to be quite an impressive young man, as far as first impressions were concerned. Kerri knew first impressions usually were just that, first impressions. Oh well, no time to think of him right now; she still had a couple of loans to go over before sending them for approval, she always went over her work several times before sending them for approval, just in case she missed anything, and it had paid off; a couple of times she found she had left a couple things out of the files that should have been included. She knew it was easy to miss something even for someone who had processed so many loans as she had, so she always went over the files several times. Kerri was just closing the last file when there was a knock on the door, and Gina stuck her head in.

Gina said, "I know you wanted to talk to me and it's getting late and I am going to have to be leaving soon so could we talk now."

Kerri looked at her watch and couldn't believe it was past the time to leave and said as much to Gina.

Gina said, "Well, I waited because I wanted to have a private conversation with you."

"Well, of course I don't mind, you know you are much a friend as you are a secretary or more so."

When Gina had taken a seat Kerri asked, "Gina what is going on with you lately? It's not like you to be late to work all the time, and you have been very distracted, are you ok?"

"Well Keri, I have met someone and I believe he is the one, if you know what I mean.

"You mean, you have met the man you are going to marry?" Keri knew this was very serious because Gina had not even been dating because she had been hurt so bad, she had decided she didn't ever want to go out with anyone ever again, and that had been about four years ago, and as far as Kerri knew, Gina hadn't even dated anyone that she knew of. Kerri looked at Gina with an astonished look asking, who, what when, and where?

Gina said, "If you have a few minutes I would like to talk with you."

"Well of course Gina, why don't you and I go to the coffee shop around the corner and have a cup of coffee and talk this over?"

As Kerri and Gina entered the coffee shop around the corner from the bank, there was a young man standing there and Gina greeted, "Pastor Ted, how nice to run into you."

"Gina how good to see you, is David here with you?" while Pastor Ted looked around for David.

Gina introduces her friend to Pastor Ted, "I would like you to meet my boss, Kerri Johnston."

Pastor Ted turned and greeted Kerri, "How nice to see you, I know we haven't seen each other since your parents' memorial, but Mary and I have been praying for you everyday." Gina looked back and forth at them, and then Kerri turned to her, "Gina, Pastor Ted was my parents' pastor, and I met him at my parents' funeral."

Gina replied, "I didn't realize you knew each other, Kerri you said the memorial was held when you were out of town visiting your aunt in Florida."

"Kerri, Mary and I would like to get together with you soon," said Pastor Ted and Kerri smiled at him, he then turned to Gina and said, "I will see you in church," and with that left the coffee house. A hostess came and seated Kerri and Gina took their order.

Kerri looked at Gina and said, "It seems we have more to talk about than I thought."

"Well, where do you want me to start?"

"When did you start going to church, and especially the church my parents were so involved in: you never said a word."

"Kerri, I started going to your parents church before your parents died, I actually went to a home group with them. I guess your mom and dad told you about the home group they were going to. They said they had tried to get you to go when you came home a couple of times."

"Yes, I remember what they told me about the home groups, they are small groups of people that go to church and meet in small groups, so they can get to know each other and pray for one another, and get ministered to because in a big church it's hard for the pastor to know and minister to everyone, does that pretty much sum it up?"

"Yes, but I don't think you knew they were the leaders of that group."

Kerri had tears in her eyes and said, "I guess there's a lot of things I didn't know or understand."

"Kerri I am so sorry to bring all this up, and I know how upset you get when your parents are mentioned; I have tried to make sure that didn't happen, I have always shied away from every subject that would bring your parents up. I don't like to see that pain on your face Kerri, and I am hoping it will get easier over time.

"I am so sorry you have felt you couldn't even talk with me, and that you knew my parents and went to their church. How come this had never come up before?"

"Well, because you see, when I was going to their home group, they ask us to pray for their daughter. When you first started working here and I realized who you were; I was promoted to be your secretary. I didn't want to bring anything up about your parents so soon after everything that had happened. I am so sorry, I hope you are not very upset with me.

"Gina, I am in no way upset with you; I am stunned that there was so much going on around me that I didn't catch or notice." Gina tried to shift the topic into something lighter and asked, "Now Gina, tell me who is David?"

Gina blushed and then answered, "Well, David is the most wonderful man in the world, and I am going to marry if and when he asks me."

Beginning of a Revelation

Kerri entered her townhome and looked around and thought she needed to clean. She had been so busy, since their talk at the coffee shop, she and Gina had hardly had time to talk. Gina had been so involved with church and David, and Kerri had to learn some of the new loan guidelines that had been passed, she barely have had time to clean, shop, or anything. She had been living on takeout, she hadn't had a lot of time to do anything other than work and come home and flop.

When Kerri thought about the conversation she and Gina had at the coffee shop, she was still shocked and surprised, and thought it was truly amazing that the whole time she an Gina had been working together, she had never mentioned that Gina knew her parents, went to their church, or anything about her young man David Connors. Gina seemed to really be headed for the altar with David and that is all she seemed to want to talk about since the coffee shop.

Kerri had learned how Gina and David met. David had been going to the same church for about a year before they met. David was involved in the music department; he played the keyboard, and helped lead praise and worship. One night at one of the group meetings at her parents' home, the praise and worship leader couldn't come and they asked David to fill in for him. David liked the home group so much, he decided to keep going to that particular group, and he and Gina just started getting to know each other.

Kerri thought she would see an engagement ring on Gina's finger any day. Kerri just hoped Gina didn't get hurt; she knew first hand how that felt. She didn't want to go thinking about that right now. Kerri thought she would take a time off tomorrow, and try to clean a little. The next morning, her cell phone was ringing and she got to it just as the last ring was sounding. She answered just a little out of breath and said hello. There was a hesitant voice on the other end saying, "This is Mary Jackson, Pastor Ted's wife, do you remember me?

"Yes, can I help you?"

"Pastor Ted and I are getting together a dinner party for next week, and we would like you to come; we are going to be discussing about doing something in your parents' honor; we would like for you to be involved."

Kerri asked, "Could you tell me a little bit about it?"

"Well, it is something we have been kicking around awhile. We would like to start a help ministry in their honor, you know, where people can come and get help with food or clothes, help with a utility bill, or help in general. Kerri your parents helped anyone and everyone who came their way; they always talked about doing this themselves, and was going to start on it when they got back from Israel. Anyway, we feel the Lord wants us to establish. This as a ministry in their name, and we would like for you to be involved."

Kerri was dumbfounded. Since her parents' death, she had learned more and more about them. Since their death, she was beginning to feel she didn't know them as well as she thought she had, then she realized she was still holding the phone. She answered, "Oh yes, I would love to come thank you. When is it?"

"It's two weeks from yesterday, on Friday evening at seven o'clock and it is casual."

"Thank you, I will put it on my calendar."

"Oh good, I am looking forward to seeing you again."

Kerri hung up the phone, and started cleaning and putting her home in order. Kerri took a quick shower and ran to the grocery store to pick up a few things. She decided to stop by and pick up some Chinese on the way home, and as she was waiting for her order, she heard a man's deep voice behind her saying, "Hello, Kerri." Startled, she turned around and there he stood smiling down at her was Brad Kensington. He said, "It seems as if we had the same idea." Kerri blushed and said, "Pardon?" she couldn't think fast enough to know what he might be talking about. Brad answered, "Chinese take out, seems we had the same idea." Kerri smiled and then said, "Yeah, I guess we did."

Brad shifted the topic, "I have everything you asked for and all the papers filled out. I just haven't had a free minute to get back to the bank in the last few weeks, and I have been very busy getting everything up and running."

"Well, give us a call and set something up with Gina and we will see what we can do."

"Ok I'm looking forward to the dinner at Pastor Ted's and Mary's in a couple of weeks." Kerri didn't know what to say and just smiled and said, "Yeah me too." Kerri didn't know what Brad Kensington had to do with the dinner at Pastor Ted's; he must be building something for them or yes its something. Kerri's order was ready and said good-bye to Brad, "It was nice to see you again" to which Brad replied, "It was nice to see you again to and I'll be looking forward to seeing you at the dinner."

Kerri thought, *Oh great I wasn't nervous enough about going to that dinner, now I really will be nervous. Oh well, I can think about that later. Now for some good Chinese, and a movie and some much needed rest. I probably need to go to church tomorrow.* Everyone she knew and or was meeting seemed to be going there. Living Faith Church seemed to be the place to be. Well, she really needed to rest tomorrow, well she would try to go one day. Kerri knew something was stirring in her soul, but didn't want to stop, and examine it right then.

Peace in the Midst of the Storm

Friday morning after running into Kerri the previous Saturday night, Brad had two meetings that morning for different reasons: one was for permits to build for the church project he was working on, and one was for the membership to the chamber of commerce. Brad also had two meetings that afternoon: one with the better business bureau, and the other with Liberty National Bank loan department and Kerri herself. Since running into Kerri the past Saturday evening, he had not been able to get her off of his mind. Brad kept trying to get her off of his mind, but she kept coming up and he didn't know why. Brad was looking forward to meeting with her even though he wasn't admitting it to himself. The day went fairly quickly and before he knew it, it was time for his meeting with Kerri. When he entered the office, he saw Gina as she looked up and smiled at him he said, "hi Gina." Since meeting her a few weeks before, he had been getting acquainted with her and David at church and at home group meetings. She looked up and said, "Hi Brad, Kerri asked me to take everything you brought today, so she could go over it. Do you want me to make copies of the originals, so you can take them with you?" Brad apologized for not making copies of the originals before he came and Gina replied, "That is all right Brad, I don't mind at all. Kerri asked me to make sure everything was here and it looks like it is. She said she would let you know when she heard anything, or if we needed anything else from you." Brad looked at Gina and she could tell he was disappointed. He asked her, "You mean I am not meeting with her today?" Gina had to work hard not to giggle and she said, "No, Kerri had to go somewhere on business for the bank but she will let you know when she gets an answer for you." Brad said, "Ok I will be waiting for the call thank you for everything Gina and he turned and left." Brad finished up doing all his errands and he was really tired, so he just went and grabbed a pizza, went home, took a shower and only ate a slice of pizza. He had just started watching sports news when his cell phone rang; it was Pastor Ted and he told Brad he was sorry for calling him and he knew Brad had had a long day, but there was an emergency and needed his help.

Brad asked, "What can I do to help?"

Pastor Ted replied, "I need someone I can trust to go and talk with Miss Johnson, I know you have been talking to her about a loan, but I trust the Lord in you to deal with this situation."

"I don't mind talking to Kerri, but what am I supposed to be talking to her about"

"Well I am glad you are on a first name basis with her that will help; you see, Gina and David have been in a horrible car accident tonight and Gina is Kerri's best friend and employee and with all she has been through, I didn't want to just call her, and I need to be at the hospital."

"Oh no, how bad is it?"

"I don't know for sure; I know that David had asked Gina to marry him tonight and she said yes and they had called Mary and I to tell us and were very happy. I can't believe this, I just talked with Gina this afternoon"

"Okay Pastor, I will get going and I'll also be praying for Gina and David.

"I know I will probably see you at the hospital because I am sure Kerri will want to be there.

When Brad pulled up to Kerri's town home to which Pastor Ted had given him the address; he went up and knocked on the door, and a few minutes latter he heard footsteps. He called out in a loud voice, so she could hear him through the door, "Kerri it's Brad Kensington, Pastor Ted sent me over. There has been an accident."

Kerri opened the door and said, "Why, what has happened?"

"David and Gina has been in a bad car accident and are in the hospital and I am here to take you to the hospital."

Kerri said, "Ok, Brad, I'll go get dressed it will only take me a minute." When Kerri left the room to go and get dressed, Brad looked around the room and thought Kerri really knew how to put a room together. It wasn't long until Kerri was ready to go. When he had helped her into his truck, Kerri asked him, "Do you know anything about the accident?" and he said, "No, Pastor Ted and Mary didn't know that much, but were on their way to the hospital. David and Gina had called them earlier and told them they were engaged."

Kerri said, "Oh I hope they are ok."

"We can pray."

Kerri didn't even question Brad's words who was also reaching out for Kerri's hand. She put her hand in his and he started praying for Gina and David and that is the way they stayed all the way to the hospital.

When they entered the hospital, they asked where to go and was sent to the intensive care unit and when they got there, they saw Pastor Ted and Mary and a few other people in prayer. Pastor Ted said the chapel filled up and people started praying in the hall; the doctor has not come out yet but is expected to come out soon. Kerri and Brad made their way down the hall to the chapel, and when Brad opened the door for her to proceed, she saw that Pastor Ted was right, the chapel was full to overflowing, but she also noticed that these people were all praying out loud, and you could tell there was an urgency about the way they were praying. Brad and Kerri did find a place to kneel, and Brad took Kerri's hand again, which to Kerri felt as natural as it could be. Brad bowed his head and started praying and Kerri followed Brad's lead and she prayed and said, "Lord, I don't know exactly what to say, please help my friend and her fiancée; she is such a wonderful person, and has been such a good friend to me. Lord please make everything right in her life."

Brad and Kerri sat there and prayed for about thirty more minutes until they heard the door open, and Pastor Ted say, "Gina was awake and going to be ok, but that David was still touch and go." Pastor Ted came up to Kerri and said, "Gina would like to see you." Kerri and Brad followed Pastor Ted back to ICU and Brad waited outside the door with Pastor Ted while Kerri went in to see Gina.

Kerri looked down at Gina and the poor little thing looked so small and helpless laying there, her beautiful blond hair was still matted with blood from the accident and her arm was bandaged up and was hooked up to an IV. Gina must have sensed her presence in the room because her big brown eyes popped open and Kerri could tell she had been crying. Gina said, "I am so sorry to get you out at this time of night." She then chuckled and added "Kerri, I know David and I are going to be ok because God put us together we were engaged tonight; I wouldn't even let them take my engagement ring off my finger. I screamed more about them trying to take it than I did about them resetting my bones and she held up her hand to show Kerri a beautiful diamond engagement ring." By the time Gina finished talking, Kerri wanted to cry and laugh at the same time but she got hold of herself and asked Gina if there was something she could do to help her. Kerri assured her that her job would be waiting, and she was to take the time she needed to get well, then Gina asked her to go to her apartment and take care of her cat until she got out of the hospital, "Go by and feed her and clean out the litter box everyday. Her name is Sheena" and Kerri said she would, then Gina started getting drowsy and she was saying, "David and I will be ok, I know Jesus will heal us" and she fell asleep. When she was sure Gina was good and asleep she got up and went out and found Brad standing exactly where she left him. Kerri said Brad "could we go somewhere and talk?" and he said, "yea how about a cup of coffee or a cold drink" she said, "yes a cold drink would be perfect." So they went down to the cafeteria and found a table in the corner and Brad went and got them each a cold drink. When Brad sat down Kerri asked him, "Brad do you think Gina and David will be ok?" and Brad said, "Well, the doctor said that Gina was out of the woods, but David was still touch and go." Kerri said "I know, but Gina was so convinced David would be ok, it was all I could do to keep from crying and she seemed to be totally at peace about everything and just knowing David would be ok." Brad said "Well, I knew that Gina has been growing in the Lord, and so she probably does have the peace of the Lord about the situation, and faith in the Lord that everything will be ok. Gina is probably resting on the scripture in the Word that says, 'The peace of God which passeth all understanding, shall keep your hearts and minds through Christ Jesus.' Philippians 4:7 and I believe it is through Gina's faith in Jesus that she is getting that peace." About that time Brad looked up to see Pastor Ted and Mary come through the door and he stood up and asked them to join them and

Pastor Ted said, "No, I think we are going to go on home and get some rest some of the prayer warriors are going to stay and keep praying and I will call and check up on Gina and David in the morning. You guys need to go on home and get some rest also and maybe come back tomorrow afternoon." Kerri sighed and said, "Poor Gina this should have been one of the happiest days of her life." Mary said "Well, the Word says 'We know that all things work together for good to them that the love God, to them who are called according to His purpose.' Romans 8:28." With that Brad took Kerri back home and told her he would call her if he heard anything. Kerri walked into her house and went straight to bed reflecting on everything that had happened that evening.

God Answers Prayer

Kerri woke the next morning knowing she needed to get back to the hospital to be there for Gina. As Kerri was eating breakfast, she was reflecting on the previous evening. Kerri could not get over the fact that there were so many concerned people who went to the hospital to pray for Gina and David. The thing was, it was real concern on their faces; they seemed to really care and want to be there and they seemed to be willing to do anything that needed to be done.

Kerri remembered her parents talking about some scripture in the bible, something about knowing people were really of God when you see fruit or something like that, oh well she didn't know what fruit had to do with anything. Maybe she would get a chance to ask Gina or Mary later. She would ask Brad, but she was just a little too shy to do that. Kerri looked at the clock and thought she had better get moving shakin' and bakin' as her mom always said then she thought, *Oh mom I miss you so much*, well she couldn't go down that trail. Gina's mom and dad wasn't supposed to be able to get there until later in the morning, and she wanted to help Gina anyway she could. Kerri walked into the hospital and went straight to ICU, but Gina wasn't there, they had moved her to a room on another floor because she was doing so well the nurse said.

Kerri then started toward the elevator and ran into Brad and Pastor Ted and they were both grinning from ear to ear, and Brad said, "Have you heard?"

"I heard Gina has been moved to a room and I am so relieved."

"No, about David"

"No, what is it?"

"Well, after I dropped you off last night. I went home and got a couple of hours sleep, then Pastor Ted called and ask me to come and pray with him and a few others for David, so we got some anointing oil and laid hands on him and prayed. The doctor came in a little while later, and threw us out of the room, so he could run some test and find out where the problems David was having were, and then they took David down for test and then when they brought him back to ICU the doctor came to talk with Pastor Ted and he was shaking his head and said he couldn't figure out what had happened and Pastor Ted said what do you mean and the doctor said that boy was dying earlier this evening and now we can't find anything wrong with him other than some obvious bruising and he is a little sore."

"But when we left the hospital, they said he was in critical condition what happened?"

Brad was still smiling and said, "God healed him that's what we prayed for isn't it?"

Kerri laughed and said, "Well, I guess it is. I have never seen anyone God has healed before."

Brad said, "That's what the doctor said."

"Well, I guess the doctor and I have something in common; did he say anything else?"

"As a matter of fact, yes."

"What?"

"He wanted to know what time services were next Sunday, he wants to try to get off."

Kerri laughed and said, "Well, I want to go and see Gina and then see David if it's alright. Of course I am going to go and see David right now when you are finished would you like to go to lunch with me? Is Mexican ok? I haven't had anything except one slice of pizza since yesterday.

"Yes, I love Mexican.

So they set a time to meet in the lobby of the hospital and Kerri went off to see Gina and had a wonderful visit with her and got to meet her mom and dad when they came in.

Kerri told Gina to take as much time as she needed and Gina said, "No I want to get back as fast as I can because I am going to want to go on a honeymoon."

"Gina get well first, I will cover for you, and then you can still take your honeymoon."

Kerri then went in to see David and she was pleasantly surprised; she really enjoyed talking with David and felt that Gina and David would make a great couple. She told Brad that after they were seated at the Mexican restaurant around the corner from the hospital. Brad said, "Yes, it is truly wonderful to see God put two people together, and make them one; I really enjoy seeing God move in people's lives.

"I heard my mom and dad say things like that and I wish now I had listened more to what they were saying about the Bible, and the things they believed. I am afraid I hurt them terribly by not being more interested; I wish I could do some things over."

"Well, Kerri Pastor Ted and Mary and a few other people have told me a lot about your parents, and they all have said that Tom and Danne Johnson were very wonderful loving people and loved you very much and trusted the Lord with you and your life."

"Brad, I would like to ask you something about the Bible and God and I am a little embarrassed."

Brad reached over the table and put his hand on Kerri's and said, "Kerri don't ever be embarrassed about asking anything about God. Now what did you want to ask me?"

"I want to know how people get to the point that they care so much about people they hardly know that their willing to go and pray all night long for them and are willing to give their time or money, and help in the way I saw last night and with my parents and some of their friends I would see things like that while I was growing up."

"Well, Kerri those are true believers of which I am one, and we are to walk in the love of God. The Word says you will know them by their fruits. Kerri said I remember my parents talking about that, and I was just remembering something my mom said to me about it but I couldn't remember exactly what she said. Well the scripture she was probably quoting is 'Ye shall know them by their fruits. Do men gather grapes of thorns or figs of thistles? Even so, every good tree bringeth forth good fruit; but a corrupt tree bring forth evil fruit. A good tree cannot bring forth evil fruit, neither can a corrupt tree bring forth good fruit.' Matthew 7: 16, 17 and 18 and what that means is you will know them by their fruits that is what the Word says...

"You see I want to live my life for the Lord and walk in the love of the Lord. You see a lot times people walk in fear and that holds them back from what God wants to do in and through their lives, but the Word of God says that perfect love casteth out fear. Kerri some people will not give their whole lives to the Lord because of fear even though they don't realize if they would it would blow their minds what God would do in them and through them. When Jesus said you will know them by their fruits He meant those who are born again and accept Him as their Savior and Lord. You see God gave us His best He sent His only Son that whoever believed in Him would have ever lasting life.

"He doesn't want to lose anyone, he says so that none perish you see his love is for ever and ever for all eternity but our minds can't even imagine a love like that that is the reason we have to be born again because we cannot do this on our own. Jesus has already paid the price by shedding his blood and he not only paid for our salvation but he also paid for our healing. The Word says by his stripes we were healed. Just like David was healed earlier today that should be normal not unusual as Christians, we should walk in the love of God and believe in the supernatural things of God that should be as normal to us as getting out of bed and brushing our teeth."

Kerri said, "That was beautiful, the way you explained that to me and so simple. I guess I always ran from God and anything to do with God and I have some thinking to do."

"Kerri, God is not complicated he just wants us to know him learn about him, and grow in him. And the more I grow in him and know him, the more I realize I don't know him."

"Thank you Brad for talking to me about this, I have enjoyed talking with you."

"Kerri, I have enjoyed this immensely. Kerri would you like to go to church with me this evening?"

Kerri replied, "Could I take a rain check I have so much to catch up on and now that Gina will be out of commission for a little while I am really going to be busy for a little while."

Brad looked a little disappointed, but she knew he understood and that really felt good.

Feelings or God

Brad knew Kerri had been busy since she was doing her and Gina's work for the past three weeks. Gina's mom and dad had stayed and taken an opportunity to get to know their future son-in-law and to help Gina and David plan their wedding. They had decided to go ahead and get married between Thanksgiving and Christmas. What a perfect time for a wedding in Christmas Town is what everyone was saying. No one was upset about adding an extra festival to the holidays and the wedding was becoming a festival. After all, Christmas Town was somewhat of a tourist town, there were stores of every kind that specialized in a little of everything Christmas Trees, sweatshirts, china, paintings, glass blowing, art, antiques, etc. There was an amusement and water park that stayed open in the summer, a lake with swimming, boating, camping, and horseback ridding. There was something for everyone, so there was always something to do, yet the town had a coziness and family-like atmosphere. Oh, it had its problems a few people doing drugs, and a criminal element here and there, but all in all it was a great place to live and Brad had done his research and knew they were going to be adding auditoriums, hotel, and restaurants, in fact he already had a bid in on the design of one of the auditoriums and he knew he would be very busy because of the growth. He thought only God could have put him in this place where he immediately found a church home and pastors like Pastor Ted and Mary. In fact he thought he needed to call Pastor Ted and Mary and make an appointment with them about the one thing that was bothering him, he really needed to talk to them about how he was beginning to feel about Kerri and he didn't want anything to be about feelings, he had been praying for God to send a wife into his life and he wanted it to be God who sent her and only God; he had been standing on the scripture Psalm 128 Chapter 3 says your wife shall be a fruitful vine by the sides of thine house: thy children like olive plants around thy table. He knew he wanted to get to know Kerri better but he wanted to be careful and prayerful because he didn't want either one of them getting hurt or making a mistake, he wanted God's wisdom and only God's wisdom.

He was defiantly going to call Pastor Ted and Mary and make an appointment with them, so he could talk to them about praying about this. Brad also wanted to find out where Kerri was with the Lord. Brad felt as if she was really close to making some decisions about the Lord and then she was saddled with such a heavy load because of the accident.

Brad knew he needed to slow his thinking down and wait on God. He knew he only wanted what God wanted for him in every aspect of his life and he didn't know if Kerri was his or not and he didn't want to think about her if she was another man's gift, he only wanted what and who God wanted him to have in his life; his gift from God, in Proverbs it says a man who finds a wife finds a good thing. Brad decided he needed to pray and when he had been praying for a while, the phone rang. When Brad answered the phone

He heard Kerri's voice when he put the phone up to his ear. Brad looked up and mumbled to the Lord, "Please give me strength; I know you have a sense of humor, but come on," and then he heard Kerri say pardon and he chuckled to himself and said, "Oh, I was just praying, Kerri, is that you?"

"Yes, I am sorry to call you so late but I was wondering what time church service starts in the morning; I finally can relax a little because Gina is coming back Monday and I thought I would try to go to church in the morning."

"Well, church starts at ten, but why don't I pick you up at nine thirty"

Kerri said, "I didn't call to get you to pick me up."

"I didn't think you did, but would you do me the honor of allowing me to pick you up and take you lunch after church? Please?"

Kerri finally said, "I would be honored sir," and giggled and Brad smiled and said, "I will see you in the morning at nine thirty.

Kerri said, "Okay, I am looking forward to it."

Finding Fullness in God

The next morning found Kerri looking through her closet for the right thing to wear. Kerri had not been shopping since her parent's plane went down; it was always hard for her to say their death because their bodies had never been found, in a way they were not even dead to her it was just hard to imagine never ever seeing them again. ok she needed to stop this train of thought or she would be crying. Now what to wear? Finally, she settled on a very pretty ankle length black skirt and an eggshell colored quarter length sleeve sweater with tiny pearl buttons down the middle, and a black belt with a eggshell colored pearl buckle.

She didn't think it was cold enough yet to wear a jacket but she went ahead and too light sweater just in case it was cold in the church or restaurant. Then she put on a very comfortable pair of black flats, grabbed her Bible and purse and was ready to walk out the door when Brad knocked. Kerri opened the door and was taken aback a little because she had never seen Brad in a suit and he looked very handsome and she said, "Wow you look nice."

Brad was sure she didn't know what a vision she was and he finally found his voice and said, "You look very nice yourself." Brad stepped back and said, "Shall we?" and allowed her to go ahead of him while he shut and locked the door.

They got to the church in plenty of time to get good seats but Brad said he always sat pretty much in the same place. When Kerri looked around she was aware of several people giving her the once over and a few young women were really taking extra pains to see her it seemed. She was getting a little uncomfortable when she heard Gina's voice saying, "Hey, I was sure hoping you would be here today."

"I didn't know until late last night."

"Kerri, one day you will know God always knows what we are going to do before we do."

Gina said she was going to sit with her and Brad because David was going to be playing the keyboard and helping lead praise and worship. Then she noticed Kerri looking at all the young women that were trying to stare her down. Gina grabbed Kerri's arm and whispered in her ear, "Don't pay any attention to them, do you hear me? you are exactly the place you are supposed to be."

Kerri looked at Gina and smiled and said ok. Then the music started and the praise and worship was beautiful the praise was very happy and exciting praising God with words like awesome God, wonderful, and great you could tell that people were very excited about praising God and then the worship started and Kerri looked up at David and he looked as if he was in another world and the worship music was the most beautiful music she had ever heard and then Kerri closed her eyes and for the life of her could not hold back the tears and then Kerri was lost and in another place a heavenly place, she didn't know how she got there but didn't care she just wanted to stay there she didn't ever want to leave that place she felt such peace, love and joy all at one time she almost couldn't contain it.

It was as if she went to heaven and she was listening to the angels sing and she just wanted to stay where she was forever, and then it was so quiet you could hear a pin drop and then a voice that sounded as strong and clear as it could be not of this world and it said You do not know the time or the hour this is the time to get your house in order I am coming for my bride without spot or wrinkle and there is much I have in store for you, things that eye has not seen nor ear heard and will be revealed in the perfect time.

Kerri was afraid to open her eyes she was shaking so hard and she didn't realize she was crying and Gina reached over and put her arm around her and held he for a moment and then Brad reached out to steady her and helped her sit down. Then Pastor Ted stood up and brought the most beautiful message of God's love and how God's forgiveness covers every sin no matter what you have done that his love is all sufficient and how he will comfort lead guide and direct you. He has a perfect plan for your life and if we ask Him he will show us every step we are to take in Him and that our footsteps are ordered by him.

When the music started again Gina asked her if she would like to go get prayer and they would go get Mary to pray for her. Being a little shy she looked at Brad and he smiled down at her and said go ahead I need to go and speak to Bill about something anyway he thought she would be more comfortable with Gina and until he knew for sure he didn't want to be to intimate because that could be confusing for them.

Kerri smiled back at him and followed Gina down front. Mary had seen them coming and met them at the altar, Mary asked, "Kerri, how can I help you?"

Kerri said, "I want everything in my life that Pastor Scott was talking about."

Mary asked Kerri, "Have you ever asked Jesus into your heart?"

Kerri said, "No, I haven't prayed much at all until recently."

Mary asked, "Kerri do you want to ask Jesus into your heart?"

"Yes."

"Kerri, the Word of God says For God so love the world He gave His only begotten son that whoever believed in him would not perish but have everlasting life John 3:16 Kerri do you believe that?"

Kerri answered yes and then Mary led Kerri in the sinner's prayer. Kerri actually felt a heaviness leave her and a peace and joy come on her when she confessed she was a sinner and asked the Lord to come into her life and said she believed He came in the flesh and died on the cross for her salvation.

They spent a few minutes talking and Mary gave Kerri some pamphlets and her phone number and told her if she had any questions to please call her. When they had finished it was as if Brad knew the perfect time to come to get her and he was standing there smiling down at him and she was smiling back him neither one of them was saying a word but they had the perfect form of communication.

Brad held his arms out and Kerri walked into them and they hugged each other and then he led her out of the church and helped her into his truck. "Keri I want to welcome you into the family of God. Let's celebrate I want to take you to this great steak house, do you like that kind of food?"

Kerri said, "Of course, it sounds great."

Kerri and Brad had a wonderful time that afternoon, she learned all about his family and listened to him tell why he wanted to be an architect and how when he was just a very small boy his mom and dad had discovered his love for drawing buildings and knew his imagination knew no bounds, so they encouraged his talent in every way they could. Even buy him a drafting table one and every thing that went with it one year for Christmas. Then they talked about Christmas and family traditions, Christmas music, Christmas decorations, shopping, holiday food, and candy. Then Brad said, "But this year the holidays will be much better because you are a child of God now and you have much to be thankful for and also Christmas is better when you know the one whose birthday it is then celebrating the season really has a reason."

Brad said one of the things that drew him to Christmas Town when he was doing his research was the name of the town and then he became aware of how the town was growing and was pleasantly surprised about all the new development that was being anticipated. They had talked about helping out at the hospital with the children on Christmas Eve and making sure there were gifts for all the children.

Then they talked of someday wanting to have children of there own. Kerri thought about the days events as she lay in her bed trying to go to sleep but then she realized she needed to start getting to know her Lord and Savior better and he got out of bed and went to get her bible that her mom and dad had bought her many years before and she thought how happy they would have been to witness today's events and so she read and prayed and got the most peaceful nights sleep she had had since she could remember.

Past Hurts

Brad awoke the next morning with a smile on his face while thinking about Kerri and what a wonderful day they had the day before. Brad was very happy about her personal decision to follow Christ but that still did not give him the answer he was seeking so he still had to wait on the Lord to tell him, but he was pleased that they seemed to have so much in common.

After he had his shower, had a bowl of cereal, and was on his second cup of coffee, the phone rang when he answered the phone and said, "Hello," he recognized her voice and asked her if everything was ok and she said yes. Gina said, "Well I was just going over things on my desk and I found your file right where I left it before my accident."

Brad said, "Gina are you at the office already?

She said, "Yes, I was so excited I just couldn't get back to sleep after I woke up early this morning and I went ahead and came on in and started to go through things on my desk and ran across your file I don't think Kerri has even seen it."

Brad said, "Well I haven't been in a hurry and I knew she had her hands full with you out."

Gina said, "Well, I am back now and I am going to make sure she looks this over and I will go ahead and set up an appointment for you for next week, is that okay?

"Okay, how about next Thursday?

Gina asked him what time?

"How about 3:00 p.m."

Gina said, "Okay, I will set it up."

With that settled Brad told Kerri to have a nice day and hung up the phone. As soon as Brad had hung the phone up, it rang again and he answered again, it was Bill Long and he said Pastor Ted has ask him to call Brad and ask him if he could bring the preliminary blueprints and come to Bill's office for a business lunch. Bill said he was having lunch catered in so they could take their time.

Brad said that was a wonderful idea and he would get everything together, and be there at eleven. Bill said it wasn't really his idea, it was his wife's idea and she was the one who was catering the lunch. Brad laughed well that's one way for her watching your diet. Well I think a working lunch is a great idea and I have eaten your wife's cooking and I would come to lunch even if we didn't have to work. Brad hung up the phone and laughed, everyone knew how Bill's wife was always hounding him to eat right and everyone knew he would sneak around and eat behind her back to fast food places. Oh everyone knew how much they loved each other, so now everyone would rib him about his wife starting a catering business to keep an eye on his eating habits.

The next time they met, he would like to have them to his apartment and cook for them himself. He hoped all of his renovation would be done soon. Brad ran to his bedroom to grab his blueprints, he had put them on top of a wardrobe that was taller than he was to keep them from getting messed up. When he pulled them down a picture had fell to the floor and he picked it up. Well there it was again; it seemed to always be popping up and he knew he was going to have to deal with it sooner or later.

The phone rang and it was a cancellation of his first appointment of the day. Brad heard the Lord say, "No time like the present."

"Lord, what can I say? The hurt went so deep and I don't want anything to keep me from having every-thing you want me to have in my life and I thought I was way past this problem but I guess I'm not huh?" Then Brad knelt by his bed and prayed. "Lord please forgive me for carrying all this hurt around, I know that by your stripe I am healed because when you shed your blood on the cross you paid the price not only for my salvation, but also for my healing because your word says by your stripes we are healed. Your Word also says, 'He healeth the broken in heart, and bindeth up their wounds.' Psalm 147: 3 and I know you have already healed all of my wounds even the emotional ones and I know if I am ever to have a relationship I will have to face this head on, so Lord I ask you to help me and forgive me once again" and then there came such a peace he knew it had to be the Lord.

Brad felt if he was going to get to know Kerri that he would need to tell her about everything that had happened in his past life. When he had been so hurt he had allowed himself to become resentful, angry, and bitter. Then came the point that he felt justified about being unforgiving and felt it was his right which allowed every evil thing to be at his doorstep and he didn't want to ever leave a door open to the devil again. One thing he had learned, hurt people hurt people and unforgiveness begets no good thing. Brad had gone to his mom and dad's pastors to get some help when he had realized what a problem he had but he still knew he still had to work through some things, so he could keep growing in the Lord, but he felt clean to the bone after praying, however he knew the devil was out to kill, steal, and destroy, so he knew he had to put his armor on every day.

Secrets

Kerri had had a wonderful day at work and since Gina had been back things had gotten so much easier on her. She was breezing through her work she couldn't believe Gina had been back almost two weeks, and then all of a sudden the day turned sour, this had to be some kind of mistake. Kerri sat there with Brad's file in front of her, she could not believe what she was looking at, written in big bold red letters denied by FBI, and she could not believe what she was looking at. Kerri was sitting there trying to understand what it all meant.

She hadn't seen Brad for a while, he had to go back to visit his parents for a few days and he had been busy helping Pastor Ted and getting the youth center building planed. She had been looking forward to their meeting today but she sat there looking at his file and she said to herself, wasn't Brad who she thought he was? *This must be a mistake,* she thought to herself with every kind of possibility running through her mind she was so deep in thought she didn't hear Gina knock on her door and was a little startled when she looked up.

Gina thought Kerri looked rather strange and she asked Kerri if everything was alright. Kerri said yes, while discreetly covering the file on her desk with another file.

Gina hadn't seen Brad's file because it was sent directly to her and she wanted it to remain that way until she could get to the bottom of it. Gina said, "I was just looking for Brad Kensington's file and Kerri said oh I have it and Gina said I guess it must have came up while I was at lunch."

Then Gina said she heard someone come in and went out to the outer office. When Gina saw Brad had walked in, she turned around and went back to announce Brad and Kerri told her to go ahead and send him in.

When Brad entered Kerri's office she had uncovered the file and she looked up at him and down at the file and he froze he had no idea that anything would show up on his file.

He looked back up at Kerri and she was just looking at him questioningly. Brad didn't know how to begin or where to start and that is what he said to Kerri. Then Kerri said please Brad start at the beginning. Brad knew if he was ever going to have a chance with Kerri now he had to tell her everything. "Well Kerri, I do want to tell you everything. The Lord told me a couple of weeks ago but I had to go home and talk to my parents first. I never thought this would ever turn up at all it was never supposed to. The only reason I was going to tell you at all is because I wanted to get to know you better and I knew if I was going to do that I didn't want to hold anything back. I was going to ask you to come over and allow me to fix dinner for you and tell you then and I would still like to do that because this is a very long story and I would like to take my time and tell you everything, do you think you could trust me to wait until tonight after dinner for me to tell you?"

Kerri said, "Yes I think that would be better than talking here. By the way no one here has seen this but me, so don't worry about prying eyes."

"Thank you, Kerri. I promise you, it's not as bad as it seems; please trust me."

Kerri said, "Okay,"

"What time tonight and how do I get to your place? How about me coming to pick you up and then I will take you back home, can you be ready at seven?"

Kerri said, "Yes, I will see you at seven."

Secrets Revealed

Brad had went to the store that morning and purchased everything he would need to make a fabulous dinner for the evening. He was going to serve a spinach salad with pecans and cranberries, shrimp cocktail, fried grouper, rice pilaf, New York style cheese cake, sparkling water, and coffee. Everything was ready except the fish and rice pilaf which could be fixed at the last minute.

The renovation had been completed and everything looked really nice. He had the bottom floor done in stainless steel, black, and glass to serve as his office drafting room and conference room. Then there was a spiraling staircase that went to the top floor apartment, which was like going to Italy done in old world style of red brick, warm soft yellow, and chocolate. The furniture was warm plush and comfortable with a built-in gas fire place that Brad had had restored downstairs in a modern setting with a black faux front and mantle and upstairs with an Italian look because he kept the red brick. Brad had also found a long beautiful brown table with mission style chairs and beautiful Tuscany style hutch, two Italian style paintings that really pulled everything together he was very pleased with the effect.

Brad made sure everything was ready, and all he had to do when he returned with Kerri was to do a couple of finishing touches. Brad got to Kerri's at seven on the dot and when she opened the door, she was ready to go she had a beautiful ankle-length white coat on, Brad thought all that girl needed was some angel wings. They got back to Brad's and after he took her coat she sniffed and said something smells wonderful and then she looked at the place, she felt as if she had just went to Italy and she was astonished when she noticed the office downstairs and she thought it was nice enough for an office but this was very and pleasantly unexpected.

Brad saw her face and said, "The downstairs I wanted plain because I want people to have their own ideas of how they want things and not be influenced by anything else however, this is my style"

Kerri replied, "This is beautiful and I don't think I have ever seen a table set so beautiful." Brad even had two wine glasses with sparkling white grape juice set in an ice bucket, she knew Brad's hobby was cooking, but she thought he had outdone himself and told him so.

Brad said, "Thank you now please be seated,"—and he pulled out her chair for her, poured some sparkling white grape juice in her glass and then left and returned with a breadboard with warm homemade bread, a knife, and butter—"Please, would you mind slicing the bread while I do some finishing touches?"

Kerri cut the bread and thought to herself, *This guy is too good to be true* but remembered he still hadn't told her what the file was about. When Brad returned he sat down and took Kerri's hand and started praying and he thanked God for the food and for their time together and asked the Lord to help him tell Kerri about his past and help her understanding.

Then Brad served Keri her first course and they enjoyed the whole meal and just talked about their likes and dislikes and some of the places they would like to visit someday. Kerri told Brad the meal was exceptional and she had enjoyed it immensely, but she needed to allow some of her dinner to settle before she had desert, so Brad said, "Why don't we go into the living area and get comfortable and I will bring in some coffee."

When they were settled and comfortable in front of the fire place and since it was the first cold day of fall, the fire was very inviting. Brad went and got the coffee tray and service and poured her a cup, he asked her if she took cream or sugar and she said no she liked her coffee black and he said, "Oh good, something else we have in common."

Then after Brad was seated, he turned to her and said, "Okay, Kerri please let me tell you this story without interruption, okay?"

Kerri nodded her head yes.

"Kerri, I have come a long way in my life but not without the Lord's help." He reached out and picked up an eight by ten picture that had been turned upside down on the side table and handed it to her and in the picture were two very pretty girls, one was a dark blond thick straight hair with a beautiful smile and a look of confidence that said, yeah I have the world by the tail, and the other actually could be described as beautiful, she had a long, full dark hair was tiny and petite and looked as if she had a secret.

Kerri studied the pictures for a few minutes and she said, "They are very pretty girls."—and gave Brad a questioning look.

Brad then sat back in his chair and lowered his head and had his fingertips together and when he spoke, there was with a catch in his voice. He looked a thousand miles away and he said, "The blond was my sister, Lucinda was her name and we called her Luce and the brunette was my high school girlfriend Kendra Wilson, who I cared a lot about." Pointing to the picture he said, "That was taken at the beginning of my senior year, you see my sister and I were fraternal friends and we were very close and Kendra was also her best friend. We went everywhere together, we were always together on the weekends, we went swimming, horseback riding, tennis, frisbee, cards, and monopoly. We played, studied, ate, we did everything together.

"One weekend we were bored and decided to go to a senior party out in the country away. We all piled into my old 1965 powder blue Chevrolet, now that car was built like a tank, let me tell you and I was very proud of that car. The evening was beautiful, warm, and we were very excited about prom, and would be starting college in the fall, and we're talking about our plans. I have went over that evening so many times, and if I could change it, I would have a million times by now. I was a pretty good kid, oh I drank a little once in a while, but never excessive and I had not become a Christian at that time, oh I knew who Jesus was, but did not have a relationship with him. Well, I decided it would be fun to try smoking some pot, now we had never done anything like that and we all talked about it and a guy in our class had told us how good this stuff was, and we ought to go get some and try it, so before the party, I called this kid and he hooked me up with this guy and I went and picked it up.

"Now, there was not one of us who had ever smoked pot before, and we had no idea how it would effect us. After we smoked a little, we piled in my car and put the rest of the pot in a hubcap of the car and started to the party, I had never driven that particular road before, so I was trying to pay attention. It was determined later I was going about fifty-five mph, when I came around a sharp corner and there were two white horses standing in the middle of the road, and we hit them hard. They were standing in the road with there rears towards us, and when we hit them, one put his leg through the windshield and the hoof hit Kendra in the head, and she was killed instantly, and they said Lucinda was slammed into the top of the side door and hit so hard it got her instantly. I was banged up all over and bleeding everywhere, he said he had cuts a bruises but than that he didn't have anything else wrong with him but at the time he was just trying his best to help Kendra and Lucinda. He said they told him later they had died instantly so he couldn't have done anything anyway.

Brad continued, "It wasn't but a few minutes, a car came up behind him and slowed down, and he screamed for them to get some help, and they drove off and it wasn't long before he heard the sirens. When the police got there, they tried to find the horses, but couldn't, and no one would claim they even owned the horses because they were afraid of being sued because the horses were out in the first place, they could tell where the horses had skidded on their hoofs off the road but for some reason the horses had disappeared.

"The police didn't even think to check for drugs that night, or test me, or anything because the horses seemed to be the culprits; oh I knew I was high, but when the accident happened I sobered up fast, and I wasn't thinking about that at all, I even forgot about the pot in the hubcap of my car. Oh up to this day I don't know if the pot played into it or not, but I really believed it was all my fault, and blamed myself and still didn't know for sure, but I was a mess knowing what I had done, and regardless, I was driving the car that killed two people. I blamed myself, and everyone was blaming me; I could see it in their faces and hear it in their voices.

"At that point, all I wanted to do was take my own life. If it hadn't been for the pastor who preached at their funeral, I might have done just that. You see Pastor Dan Cummings was the name of the pastor, and the one who baptized Luce and Kendra. They we had gone to the church a few times and they were beginning to really know the Lord, but I was the rebellious one. Anyway with the help of Pastor Dan, I started learning about the Lord and I finally received the Lord as my Savior, but forgiveness was something I really had a hard time with. Oh, I could forgive anyone of anything with no problem, but I did not know how to forgive myself, that was the big one. Even though I had received the Lord I would not forgive myself, and so I became angry, bitter, and selfish. I started thinking only of myself; believe me, hurt people, hurt people. I was not hurt by others, I was hurting myself by not forgiving myself, so there was no one in my way but me.

"I started college and I worked very hard, buried myself in my studies because I had something to prove. At the start of my third year of college is when everything came to a head. The police never investigated the accident other than these horses; they didn't take any blood test from me, or the girls and had closed the case, but when the car was being crushed because it had sat in the wrecking yard all this time; they removed the things that could be sold from wrecked cars, like hubcaps and different things.

"Well, I had forgotten all about putting that bag of pot in the hubcap of the car. When they took the hubcaps off the car to get it ready for salvage, the bag fell on the ground and the man that was working that day was a Christian, and he thought it was his duty to give it to the authorities. Well, they sent an investigator to go out to the wrecking yard, and lo and behold that opened the case back up, and then they informed Kendra's farther and my parents of their findings, and they came and got me from school and questioned me, and I told them the whole story because I had been dealing with it for so long, I was relieved to get it off my chest.

"Well you see the accident happened just over the state line, and that brought the feds into it, and there was a major investigation done, but they couldn't find enough evidence to even bring charges against me. At the preliminary hearing, the judge said it was very self-explanatory to him and everyone who looked at the case, that even if I had been high at the time it was the fault of the horses so the case was closed. Even though the case was closed, I was back where I started from, until Pastor Dan entered my life again. I had taken a year off from college to deal with everything; Pastor Dan got me to attending church, and it was during one of his sermons, I finally got it, and I really accepted the Lord and wanted to know him and not just about him.

"Pastor Dan preached a sermon that he said the Lord gave him after he had preached at a young person's funeral and he started thinking about the young man who had been killed in a car accident. Pastor Dan knew the young man and his family quite well, and had led the young man to the Lord himself. On the way home, he started thinking how hard it was to preach funerals that you didn't know if the individual was saved or not. Pastor Dan said, 'Let's pretend,' and to make the demonstration come to life, he had one of the funeral homes in town bring a casket to the church the night before, and he asked them to please roll it out, and he said, 'Oh now, I have your attention' when everyone gasped, even the Sunday morning sleepers opened their eyes.

Then he said, 'Let's pretend that there is a young man in this casket,' it was the evening before the funeral and there was a reporter standing in front of the casket, asking questions to everyone who came up to the casket, and you could hear their answers. First, a man comes up and the reporter introduces himself, and he said, 'I would like you to tell me, did you know the deceased well?' And the man said, 'No, I just knew him when he would come in to buy something. I noticed, he would always say, hell.' Then the reporter ask, 'Did you know if he was a Christian?' And the man said, 'No, I didn't know anything about him at all.' The reporter asked, 'So he never told you about Jesus?' and the man said, 'No,' and moved along.

Then the second man came up and the reporter asked, 'Did you know the deceased well?' The second man said, 'Oh, we would see each other at ball games, talk to each other once in a while.' And then the reporter asked him, 'Did you know if he was a Christian?' The man answered and said, 'No, we never talked bout that.' Then the third man came up and the reporter asked, 'Did you know the deceased well?' The third man said, 'Yeah, man we were family that is my cousin,' and the reporter asked, 'Did you know if he was a Christian?' The man answered and said, 'Hey man, no, we never talked about that but, I sure am going to miss him.'

Then there was a lady who came up, and she was sobbing very hard, and reached into the casket, and put her hand on the deceased hand and you could tell she really loved this person. Then the reporter asked, 'Did you know the deceased well?' The lady looked at the reporter and said, 'Yes, he is my son.' The reporter asked 'Was he a Christian?' The lady started crying so hard and said, 'I hope so; I don't know for sure; we never spoke of it.'

Everyone in the church had tears in their eyes including me, Pastor Dan said, 'We need to ask ourselves, if something were to happen to us; if the acquaintance at the gas station we see everyday knows if we went to heaven or not; if the neighbor nextdoor, the person you see everyday would know if you went to heaven; if our family members would know if we went to heaven; and if our own mother would know if we went to heaven. You see church if you are a Christian, then everyone we meet should know it, because it is our responsibility to tell others about Christ. Well by the time the service was over, even before the altar call, the altars were full and I was one who truly accepted the Lord and even though I still had things to work through I knew I wanted to get to know him, and accept his forgiveness and be able to forgive myself for every thing.'

"Then I went back to school, and decided I not only had to do well for Christ, but for Lucinda, Kendra, and myself as well. Kerri, I wanted to tell you everything, and keep nothing from you because I really like you and I want to get to know you. Anyway, after I finished college, I went back home and I wanted to get a loan, and I went to our local bank and filled out the papers, but they turned me down not because I had bad credit. I didn't have any credit, and I was working for a small firm, I was making fairly good money, but the only loan I could get was one I had to put up half the collateral and I didn't have any.

"I had a friend I had went to school with and I trusted. I had no reason not to, and we were talking one day and he said, oh I can get you a loan, don't worry, and he brought me some papers to fill out and I did. Everything looked legit to me and I got the loan, and I moved-in the house and fixed it up a little, kept it about a year, and I was getting ready to put it on the market. When I was watching the news one night, Lo! and behold there was my loan officer friend being led out of the bank in handcuffs. And then the reporter said, it had something to do with the veteran's administration. Well, I felt sorry for the guy, but didn't think it had anything to do with me. However, the next day the FBI showed up at my house and said my loan was attained fraudulently, that this loan officer had been forging VA certificates to get loans through without money down. Well, I had to get a lawyer and I finally got out of the mess, and they said they knew I had nothing to do with it, but I guess they haven't cleaned the whole thing up, so I will have to give my lawyer a call to get this part straightened out.

Kerri said, "*Wow!*"

Brad said, "One more thing Kerri, I would have told you about all this eventually, if this had not come up when it did because I would like to get to know you better, if you would let me."

Kerri said, "Yes, I would like that very much."

Ministry of Helps

Kerri wished she had opened up about her past the other night, but she didn't want to bring it up, especially after what he told her. But she had enjoyed being with Brad and listening to him, she was always very comfortable around him. She had asked him to come to her house for dinner the next Friday evening. She had asked for Friday off, so she could clean and prepare food for the evening but Thursday afternoon she started feeling bad and finally had to call Brad and cancel for the next evening. Thursday evening she heard a knock on her door and went to answer it. Kerri cracked the door open just so she could peek out, and there stood Brad loaded down with containers and bags she was so astonished she forgot she was in her pajamas and opened the door to let him in. Then she remembered and she grabbed her blanket and wrapped herself in it.

Brad came in and put all the containers and bags down on the table and unpacked everything he had made homemade chicken soup and brought medicine, saltines club soda, tissues, canned tomato soup, orange juice, flowers, magazines, movies, and a couple of books he thought she might be interested in. Kerri was very groggy and she felt so bad, Brad put her back to bed and put everything up, and then he went to ask her if she wanted to eat some soup, and she said, no all she wanted to do was get some sleep, and Brad said he would be back by in the morning, she didn't have enough strength to even argue the point.

Kerri slept all night, she had just gotten up and went to the bathroom when she heard a knock on the door, and standing beside Brad was a very attractive woman in her late forties or early fifties with short red hair and nursing outfit on. Kerri looked at them puzzled and Brad said, "Kerri, this is Ruby she is here to help." Kerri tried to argue but didn't have the strength. Before she realized what had happened Ruby had directed her to the bathroom and was drawing her a bath, she got Kerri to tell her where her clean linens, towels, under clothes, and pajamas were, and while she was running the water she put some special bath salts in that smelled heavenly.

Ruby went out and Kerri stepped into the tub it was the absolute perfect temperature. When Kerri had soaked and bathed she was about to get out of the tub when Ruby knocked and stuck her hand in the door to lay Kerri's things on the vanity, and when she stepped out, she looked around, Ruby had straightened up, changed the bed sheets, dusted and vacuumed; everything looked so nice but Kerri knew she needed to get back into bed because she was still to sick to be up. All at once Ruby was at her side helping her back into bed, and then went out of the bedroom and closed the door.

When Kerri woke again she was aware of someone in the bathroom, and was to tired to care, she turned over, and then Ruby was standing over her with some medicine and asking her if she would like some soup. Gina said, "You know, I am kind of hungry," and with that Ruby went out and brought a tray back with soup, crackers and club soda. After Kerri went to the bathroom and brushed her teeth, she went back to bed and was only awakened when Brad touched her, and he said, "I just wanted to tell you I was here to take Ruby home."

Ruby stuck her head in and Kerri said, "Ruby, you are so precious, thank you so much for all of this, but I want to give you some money for all you have done."

Ruby said, "I didn't do that much," she said a cleaning crew came in. "A cleaned present from Gina and David and I just was doing what my ministry is doing, helping people in need."

Kerri told Brad, she didn't care how he gave the money to Ruby, but she wanted Ruby to have it, Ruby heard her and she said, "I tell you what, this is a ministry and I have started a ministry of helps, and we go and help everywhere we can, and I try to use the abused women and I give them money to help, so if you want to donate to that you can."

Kerri asked Brad to get her purse for her, and told him where it was, and she only had three hundred dollars cash, and gave all of it to Ruby, and told her she hadn't been taken care of like that since her mother, and she said she couldn't believe how comfortable Ruby made her feel. Kerri told Ruby, she would like to become a permanent part of Ruby's ministry, and Ruby had tears in her eyes and said thank you.

Kerri said, "If I wasn't sick, I would want a hug." and Ruby said she didn't care she wasn't afraid of a silly bug and gave Kerri a bear hug. Then Brad left to take Ruby home, and she didn't see him until the next Sunday.

The Threat

Kerri looked forward to Sunday and going to church, she had been sick and she wanted to make sure she was well before she got out to go anywhere or went back to work. Kerri had just about decided Brad wasn't interested in her, the way she was beginning to think he was, maybe he decided they didn't have enough in common and was just a very nice person who had entered her life for a moment. Kerri said to herself, it didn't matter, she knew she needed to get to know the Lord better and wanted to go to church and get to know people.

Kerri wanted to make sure that she was going in the right direction, she may already be headed in the right direction, but she wanted to make sure. Kerri had selected what to wear for church the next day, and set her alarm and was about to go to bed when the phone rang, and it was Brad he said, "Kerri, I am sorry, I am sorry, I haven't called but about the time I thought you might be well enough, I got busy with Bill and

Pastor Ted on the design for the youth building, but I wanted to get together with you for lunch if you will go with me."

Kerri said, "Brad you have done so much for me, if it would be alright I would like to fix lunch for you."

"You talked me into it, can I bring anything?"

"No."

Brad asked her, "Kerri, can I at least come and pick you up for church in the morning?"

Kerri answered, "I would be honored."

When she hung up, she knew she had to get her menu planned for lunch the next day. Kerri decided she needed to go to an all night supermarket and got dressed went to the supermarket and got what she needed and hurried home, reset the alarm and went to sleep when the alarm went off, Kerri got up, and made the salad, and put it in the refrigerator, and then put a couple of steaks in to marinate, put the soft drinks in the refrigerator, made some tea, got the potatoes ready to put in the oven when they came in.

Kerri put the charcoal on the grill, and had it ready to light. Kerri went to get dressed, and she didn't have to wait long when she heard Brad knock on the door. Kerri answered the door, and Brad said, "*Wow,*"

Kerri said, "Well I know I look better now than I did the last time you saw me."

Brad said, "You looked just as beautiful then."

Kerri laughed and she really looked beautiful she had chosen a fitted ankle length dark blue pin stripe skirt and matching jacket with a red satin shirt under it.

Kerri said, "I know something is wrong with you now but okay."

Kerri hadn't been to the church since she accepted the Lord as her savior. Kerri had been reading her bible and praying, she took her conversion very seriously. When they entered the church, they went and sat in the same place they sat before. Some of the people got up and welcomed Kerri back even some of the young women, but there were two who came over and gave Brad a hug, and one kicked her and the other said, "Well I didn't think you would be back." and did it in such a way as Brad couldn't see or hear what had happened.

The girls went back to their seats and stared a hole through Kerri. Kerri did not understand what she had done to receive such hostility from the young woman. Well she probably needed to speak to Brad even though they were not dating, but she would never want to hurt someone not the way she had been hurt. Kerri forgot all about the girls as she entered into praise and worship. Kerri had been listening to some of the praise and worship music, and was so caught up in the spirit that she did not realize she was actually singing along and going deeper in worship.

The Holy Spirit fell on her and she was deep in worship in a place she had never been, and did not want to leave. How beautiful , how glorious, how marvelous, and how wonderful is your name, *oh Lord* was the words everyone was singing to the Lord and Jesus you are everything and thank you for being everything to me. Kerri felt as if she was in heaven that she was with the angels praising the Lord she did not want to stop worshiping for a moment and she said to herself she had to make time for this kind of worship at home she felt like a little girl that could run get in her daddy's lap and he would hold her love her and call her his perfect little girl.

Kerri enjoyed the service so much she wanted to shout which astounded her because she was a very quite person normally. After church was over, Kerri saw Gina headed her way and they used to have lunch together once in a while, but had not been able to in the last couple of weeks because every spare moment Gina had, she was using to get ready for the wedding in fact she needed to ask Gina when she wanted her to go get fitted for her dress, Gina had asked her to be her maid of honor. About the time Gina was ready to speak to her, the girl who had spoken ugly to Kerri came between them and interrupted, she was trying her best to keep Gina's attention by rambling non-stop about nothing for a while and then when Gina had had enough.

Gina reached around the girl and said, Kerri I need to talk to you about your dress for the wedding. Kerri and Gina discussed the wedding and the dress and a few other things and she looked Brad's way and noticed the girl was standing as close as she could get to Brad and was hanging on to him, she looked away and Gina leaned over and whispered in her ear, you have nothing to worry about that guy is crazy about you, so don't worry. Kerri looked up at her and said it shows that much and Gina said only to me where you're concerned, but to the whole church where he is concerned about that time she looked in Brad's direction and the girl looked right through her and if looks could kill she would be dead.

Brad looked down at Kerri and if she could have read his thoughts, she would not have had a second thought about any other girl. Brad bent down and whispered in her ear and said, "Are you ready to go?"

She said yes.

"I hope you have a big lunch planned, and I hope you like football, we have our first season game today, and it comes on in about a half an hour."

Kerri was grinning from ear to ear, and said, "I was hoping the same thing."

Brad and Kerri had a wonderful time that afternoon they had salad, steaks, baked potatoes, and apple pie alamode. Brad said, "What a meal, I can see you know your way around a kitchen also."

After the game was over, Brad said he had to go home because he had to get ready for work the next day. Kerri finished cleaning up after he left, and got ready for bed thinking how wonderful she felt and how at peace she was. If Kerri had known what was going on across town, she would not have been so comfortable because the two young women she had encountered earlier in the day were cutting her to pieces, and the only reason was jealousy, that green eyed monster had raised his ugly head and was trying to start trouble, but the Lord was watching over this little one and as she prayed, the angels were sent forth to take care of the enemy and his devices.

American Embassy

Gina knocked on Kerri's door and asked if she could come in, and Kerri said yes I want to talk to you for a few minutes anyway. Well I need a break anyway, so how about me going to get us a cold drink, and we'll both take a break. Gina went and got a couple of diet drinks and a package of peanut butter crackers for them to split and they sat a talked for a few minutes. Kerri asked Gina, "Can David tell me where to get the music like we sing at church,"

"Yes but let me download some for you to your MP3 player."

Kerri said, "No Gina I want to pay for them, an artist needs to be paid for what he does, and artist does not even start to describe David he has such a gift it is amazing."

"God really uses him to help get everyone into such a place of worship, it is amazing."

"Kerri the Lord wants to open that place up to all of us he wants us to enter in. He longs for us to enter in, so he is always there waiting with open arms. He wants us to communicate with him and tell him we love him. He is always ready and waiting do you know what I mean?"

Kerri said, "Well, I think I am beginning to. I pray that boy never stops what he is doing."

"Kerri, I know you just recently came to the Lord, but has anyone talked with you about being water baptized, or being baptized in the Holy Spirit?"

Kerri said, "I remember my mom and dad talking about it, but I wasn't paying much attention to them at the time because I wasn't interested in anything they were saying at the time."

"Well I know that this is not the time to discuss it, but I would like it if you and Brad and David and I could all get together this weekend."

Kerri said, "I would love to, but I cannot speak for Brad."

Gina replied, "I will ask him, but why don't we go ahead and plan to get together at our new apartment, we went ahead and rented on and moved in, so I could start setting up housekeeping then after the wedding we just go home. It was nice of Pastor Ted and Mary to ask David to stay with them until we are married."

Kerri said, "Are you sure they aren't just keeping an eye on you guys?"

She laughed and Gina laughed, and Gina continued, "Just plan on having dinner we will order in and have a wonderful evening and we will also talk about water baptism and the baptism in the Holy Spirit, but first I will make sure Brad can come and then I will let you know."

Gina makes sure Brad wants to come, "I don't want to be the reason, he breaks up with anyone if you know what I mean? Kerri, if you think that girl has anything to do with Brad, you are way off base, she tried the same thing when David and I started dating and I wanted to cream her until I spoke with Mary and found out she was a very hurt girl and needs lots of prayer and lots of love, so let's pray for her she needs lots of healing."

Kerri said, "Okay," then the phone rang and it was back to work for Gina and Kerri. A couple of hours later Kerri's boss called and said Brad's loan was approved. Kerri was just about to put a phone call into Brad. Gina buzzed Kerri, and Kerri answered and told Gina unless it was important she was about to make an important call. Gina said well Kerri I think you ought to take this call, it might really be important. Kerri asked Gina who is it and Gina said the American Embassy in Israel. Kerri said ok, Gina put it through and come on in.

When Kerri picked up the phone she could not imagine who or why anyone would be calling her from the American Embassy in Israel. When Kerri picked up the phone she said, "This is Kerri Johnson can I help you?"

"Yes, Miss Johnson this is Ambassador Levine are you the Miss Kerri Johnson whose parent's plane was reported to have gone down and disappeared over a year ago?"

"Yes, speaking."

"Well it seems we came across some information, we would like to discuss with you."

87

Kerri asked him, "Can you tell me what this is about?"

"No, Miss Johnson not over the phone, I would like to come by your home this evening I am in town for a couple of days would that be okay."

"Yes Sir, would you like to have my address?"

"Yes, I think we have but just in case give it to me again, and your cellphone number."

Kerri gave him the information he asked for and then he told her he, and his assistant would be by at seven. Kerri hung up the phone and looked questionably at Gina and Gina said well? Kerri then told her what he said, and Gina said, "I am going home with you Kerri and furthermore, I am calling David to meet me there,"

"Gina you don't have to do that, they probably have an update on the plane and what actually happened to the plane."

"I don't care, I still want to be there and so will David, are you ok? or do you want me to drive you?"

Kerri answered, "Oh no, I will be ok, but I think I will leave a little early, if you don't mind finishing up,"

"No, I don't."

After Kerri left, she called Brad and told him and he said he would go on over, and Gina said she and David would be there later.

A Glimmer of Hope

As soon as Kerri got home, she set about cleaning up and preparing some appetizers, cheese and crackers, cookies, coffee, tea, and apple cider. It had turned much colder, and she wanted everyone to be comfortable. Kerri thought they had found her parent's bodies and was trying her best to prepare for the news she was about to receive, and even though she felt as if she had accepted their death, she still held out a small hope that they would walk through the door one day because without their bodies or plane being found, she still had a tiny spark of hope in her as unlikely as it may be. She was becoming very nervous about the ambassador's visit.

Kerri finished putting everything out and had just changed her clothes into a warm-up suit when the door bell rang. Brad was standing there with a look of concern on his face, and she said, "Gina must have called you right?"

Brad shook his head, "No but David did and he also told Pastor Ted and Mary, and they are on there way over too."

Kerri said, "You didn't have to get out; I don't know what this is about, it may be nothing."

"Do you mind that I did come?"

Kerri said, "No of course not, I am glad you're here. I just meant there may be no reason to get everyone out tonight."

"Well Kerri, I don't know about everyone else, but I want to be with you a lot more than I am anyway." and he put his arm around her, and she looked up at him, and that is all it took. She was in his arms and he was holding her, and she thought to herself, *this feels so right,* then the doorbell rang again, and Brad said, "Allow me," and he let her go and he went to answer the door and it was Gina and David.

David and Gina were loaded down with deli boxes, and Gina said we thought since everyone was just leaving work, we might bring a few things to eat since she had had already prepared some snacks and drinks there was quite a spread. Kerri said she doubted there was anything to all of this.

Gina said, "Well it is the ambassador of Israel and I feel that might be significant, and if it is nothing, no big deal, okay?"

Kerri said, "Okay, let's all just have a cup of cider and wait and see."

Pastor Ted and Mary arrived and they were all talking about what the ambassador might have found out, and promptly at seven the doorbell rang and Kerri went to answer it. Kerri welcomed Ambassador Levine and his aid, which was introduced as Joseph, Brad was standing right beside Kerri and he could take their coats, and hung them up in the coat closet, then Kerri brought them in and introduced them to everyone, and told Ambassador Levine these were all her very close friends, and he could speak freely in front of them.

After the ambassador had acknowledged everyone and been seated, he look at Kerri and said, "Now, I know you were told we never found the plane."

Kerri said yes and sat up on the edge of the couch, and Brad was sitting beside her; he put his arm around her.

Then Ambassador Levine said, "Well, we have found the plane now, and it looks as if someone had planned to land it there. The plane was camouflaged in such a way that our satellites didn't pick it up, but it looks as if the plane was landed, and the baggage removed because there is no sign of a body anywhere, no blood, nothing. It looks as if the plane landed and the baggage was taken off and the passengers walked off."

Kerri said, "Ambassador, are you saying my parents may sill be alive?"

The ambassador said, "I don't know if they are or not, but it sure is a possibility, but now there is a chance it could end the same way, but we didn't want you watching a news report and finding this out."

Kerri asked the ambassador, "Are they still looking?"

The ambassador answered, "I promise you the US and Israel are going to do all we can to find out what happened to those passengers."

Kerri was in between shock and amazement and she was actually feeling a little faint. Brad saw, how all of this was affecting her and he held on to her tight when she stood to her feet as the ambassador and his aid Joseph stood up.

Kerri offered, "Would you like some cider or something to eat Ambassador?"

He replied, "No, we have to be going, but we will keep you informed every step of the way" and together with Kerri they started to walk to the door and the ambassador glanced at Brad and said, "No we will see our way out. Someone needs to stay with her for a while, this is a lot to absorb all at once"

Brad reassured him, "She will be well taken cared of and the ambassador and Joseph left.

Brad steadied Kerri and helped her sit back down she was shaking her head, saying I don't know what to think, and then everyone offered their support and prayers. Kerri wanted everyone to go ahead and eat, but Brad would not leave her side, he had put a lap spread around her shoulders and Gina had brought her a cup of hot apple cider. Keri sat there thinking and all of a sudden started laughing, and Brad asked her what was wrong?

Kerri answered, "There is nothing at all wrong, I have just learned that my parents may still be alive; I am going to believe and thank God. He is giving them back to me, and I am going to believe they are coming home."

Then suddenly Kerri said, "Oh! No!"

Gina asked what was wrong.

"I sold their house."

No one knew whether to get her hopes up, or not and Brad, thought it could be worse if they were in the hands of terrorist, but he wanted to help Kerri keep her spirits up, so he said I think we ought to pray, and Pastor Ted second the motion and Brad ask Pastor Ted to take the lead. Pastor Ted had everyone join hands, and started praying, Lord, "We don't know what all of this means, but we pray that if Tom and Deanne are still alive that you watch over them and keep them safe until they can get home and everyone prayed for Kerri and for the safe return of her parents."

After they had prayed Keri was famished and she said, "Let's finish up this food before you all go" and so they all ate and speculated as to what would be the outcome.

After everyone but Brad had left, Kerri told him his loan had been approved. "You can get the money by Tuesday of next week."

Brad said, "Kerri thank you so much for working so hard on it for me, but I am not sure I even want to do this with a loan now I am thinking the Lord may want me to do it with his help only I am sorry you went to so much trouble."

Kerri said, "It's alright I am none the worse for wear and I got to meet you."

Brad said, "God works in mysterious ways."

Christmas Spirit

Saturday morning Kerri woke to look out on a snow covered world. She was looking out the window and drinking her first cup of coffee and she felt lighter than she had in a long time, and happier even though this could still end the same way as the ambassador said, but she was going to do exactly as she had told everyone she was going to believe the best and believe that God would bring them home there was something inside her that truly believed what she was telling herself was true. Kerri didn't want to think about the fact if they were alive what they could be going through. Kerri knew God was taking care of them and he knew exactly where they were.

Kerri knew it was a little early, but wanted to go Christmas shopping for her parents and she loved the snow which put her in the mood for Christmas, and she loved shopping so she thought it would be fun. Oh she wished her mother were with her right now, she always had a good time with her mother and if her dad was here he would make an event out of going Christmas shopping but then again her dad made an event out of everything she remembered if her mom popped popcorn it was an event to be relished, or cutting a watermelon on a summer Saturday afternoon.

Tom Johnson was passionate about life, he enjoyed it to it's fullest and wanted everyone else to do so along with him even though it irritated her beyond belief, he would walk into her bedroom to get her up in the morning at six o'clock and turn the lights on and say rise and shine of course her mother always told her be glad it wasn't five and they would laugh. Tom Johnson had a great zeal for life, and seemed to enjoy it to its fullest, she guessed that was the reason he enjoyed telling people about Jesus because he had so much zest for life. Tom would be the first to tell people he knew it was the Lord who gave him everything even his wife and daughter, the way he told it was he grew up poverty stricken with a father who ran out on him, and his sisters and they had lived in a rundown clapboard shack without insulation, and holes in the walls.

Kerri guessed that was the reason he was like he was because he was so thankful for everything that God had done for him. He never met a stranger and was just as comfortable talking to someone standing in the middle of the highway as he was in his own home sitting in his favorite chair and he loved to give and help people. Well enough of that, I had better get my shower and get dressed because I want to get some shopping done.

Kerri was just about ready to walk out the door when the phone rang and she had to dig it out of her purse and she said hello and Brad said hello and asked her what she was doing and she told him what she wanted to do and what she had been thinking.

Brad asked, "Would you like some company?" he added, "I love Christmas shopping and Mary gave me the Christmas tags for the tree angel already where you pick a tag off the tree and buy that gift, so all the children get a Christmas present"

"Yes, she told me and I would like to buy a few myself if it would be okay."

Brad said, "I will be there to pick you up in ten minutes okay."

She responded, "Okay." and since she was already to go she watched it snow and started thinking about how her mother always enjoyed taking her to the Christmas parade and then they would go into the candy store and buy cashews and bonbons two of her mother's favorite treats. How they would always get a real tree and go pick it out and the house smelled so good with the tree smell Kerri was smiling to herself and she could almost smell that smell when she looked out the window and saw Brad pulling up.

Kerri went and opened the door about the time he got to it, so he helped her in his truck and then they made the list of stores they wanted to go to. They had a very eventful day; they hit all the stores on their list and bought a lot of the angel tree stuff. She bought her mom and dad a few things including coats and gloves.

Brad said, "You know we didn't even stop for lunch"

"I know I am starving."

"Let's pick up some take out and go back to your place and unload and wrap some of these angel tree gifts so I can take them to Mary on Sunday"

"That is a good idea, I have all the wrapping paper and tape we will need and Mary will be thrilled. Mary has been a little concerned about the angel tree since the economy downturned."

"Yes, I know but God always supplies."

Brad stopped and went in and got take out at a Chinese restaurant and when they got to her house he wouldn't let her help unload at all so she went and put some hot tea on and set out some plates on the coffee table and took all the food in and got silverware and when Brad had gotten everything unloaded they sat and had a nice dinner and just talked.

Kerri said, "I am to full to wrap presents right now and we have a ton of leftovers why don't we do this at a later date and watch a Christmas movie.

"If it's okay, could I pick you up for church in the morning?"

"Absolutely."

When they came home they would wrap the gifts and finish the leftover Chinese and so they cleaned up put everything in the refrigerator and Kerri put on a Christmas movie they moved to the couch, and Brad moved over and put his arm around her and she kind of snuggled up to him and he leaned down and kissed her and she put her arm around his neck and they kissed for a few minutes and then the kisses were getting more demanding until they both knew they were in danger-ous territory and they pulled back at the same time.

"Kerri, I think it is time we had a very serious talk."

Kerri nodded her head yes, and muted the movie.

"Look Kerri, I think we are old enough to know what can happen when a couple goes too far."

"I'm sorry."

"Wait a minute you didn't do anything, but follow my lead so I should be apologizing to you. I think we are both healthy young people and I for one am definitely looking forward to my wedding night, but I believe there is someone God has for me and I believe there is someone God has for you, and I want to make sure that the gift fits both of us before we try it on."

Kerri started shyly but finished strong, "Brad I also feel the same way even before I accepted Christ, I am a virgin and I want to be a virgin on my wedding night, you see I was taught about sex, virtue, and God's plan for marriage from a very early age. You see my mother told me a story that helped me remain a virgin until I married not that God can't forgive, but why not have the ultimate experience well you see this is about my mother, I have never told anyone but Gina, and the only reason I told her is because I felt it would help her stay chaste. You see my mother got pregnant out of wedlock and then he didn't want anything at all to do with my mother, and she knew my dad and he found out, and he wanted to marry her, he was in love with her and couldn't ever get her attention away from my birth father, well, my mom was in a spot she didn't believe in abortion and she wanted me, she said she was already in love with me, so she gave in to him and married and I was so close to nine months after they married. no one ever questioned it, she said she knows God had mercy on her, and sent my dad into her life, you see he had mumps when he was a teenager and that left him where he couldn't have children, so the Lord forgave and had mercy, but my mother said she fell in love with my dad, she always told me love is a choice not an accident."

"We only talked about this three times in my life, and my dad and I never discussed it, but I often think of how scared my mother must have been. At that time, she didn't know the Lord and she went to work in a downtown office at an oil company as a receptionist after my dad and her were married and she met this young woman there her name was Melanie and she was funny, very pretty with beautiful red hair, she talked loud, so you could hear everything she talked about and my mom would sit and listen to her talk about this church she went to, how wonderful it was, and how it was growing, and so my mom went up to her one day, and asked her if she could go to church with her and this woman said 'no I don't like you.'

"Well, my mom was devastated but she didn't say anything to my father about it and she went back to work the next day and the woman came and found her and ask her to go to lunch with her and so she took her to lunch the next day and they talk chit chat mostly but on the way back to the office the woman had one of her churche's cassette tapes of the church choir singing, and she popped it into her car cassette player and my mom said it was the most beautiful music and I didn't know what she really meant until recently.

"Anyway, my mom started crying and the woman asked her and my dad to go to church with her that Sunday and they did and they have all been best friends ever since the only one their disappearance was harder on than me was Melanie oh that reminds me I need to call her about the Ambassador coming by. I know I took time in coming to the Lord but I paid attention to my parents and what they said about marriage. Yes Brad I only want who God has for me also."

"Well, Kerri I think we both have some praying to do I believe it is very possible we have found each other but we both need to know for sure. How about us seeing a lot more of each other also?"

"Okay and then Brad left and gave her a peck on the cheek."

Thanksgiving

Brad and Kerri were becoming quite the item now they were together eighty to ninety percent of the time and no one said Brad or Kerri it was always Brad and Kerri now. Kerri was planning thanksgiving over at Brads because he had the longest table and they were both doing the cooking in fact she was getting ready to walk out the door and was headed to Brads when he called and ask if she had extra whipping cream and she said yes she would bring plenty.

On her way to Brad's she was remembering the day a few weeks before when she and Brad had went shopping and what a wonderful day she had with the gifts they had bought for the tree angel in fact Mary was amazed and wanted to know if they left anything for anyone else to buy they had bought computers, I-pods, DS games, dolls, trains, cars, board games every kind of toy known to man, coats, gloves hats. Kerri didn't think she had ever had as much fun but she didn't have time to think about all that right now.

It was only two weeks before David and Gina's wedding and so she and Brad had offered to do Thanksgiving she had made two pumpkin pies, two, pecan pies, a carrot cake, cranberry sauce, homemade rolls, and dressing. Brad was taking care of everything else. Kerri knew she had probably over done the deserts but wanted to do something to keep her mind off of her parents and to stay busy. Every one had been working hard on Gina's wedding and she and Brad thought the least they could do would be to prepare thanksgiving dinner. Pastor Ted and Mary had a brand new baby and didn't want to get out with him just yet but she had called and spoken with Gina and Gina convinced them to come on anyway.

Gina's parents had decided to come back and stay with Gina until her wedding so it would be a full house with Gina and David, Pastor Ted and Mary, Gina's parents and she and Brad. When Kerri pulled in Brad was expecting her so he ran out and started taking in boxes and bags and told her to go on in and he would get the rest. When she walked in she could not believe her eyes she felt as if she had walked into a production put on by a food TV and decorator TV when he finished bringing things in she told him this table is I am sure the most beautiful table setting I have ever seen and she looked at him and said so you're a little gourmet, and a little decorator. They were standing in the kitchen looking at each other and they were both realizing how hard it was to keep their hands off of each other when the door bell rang and he bent down and they kissed and hugged and Brad whispered saved by the bell after that they didn't have another moment alone the rest of the evening.

Thanksgiving dinner was absolutely wonderful and everyone seemed to have a good time and everyone walked away with enough food for the next day. Brad had asked her to go black Friday shopping with him and so she wanted to go home and get some sleep so she could be ready when he came to pick her up at four the next morning. Pastor Ted said as he was walking out the door four in the morning, "You both deserve each other." and his wife. "I wouldn't be saying anything, it's your turn with the baby tonight" and he groaned, Mary was breast feeding but she was freezing some so they could both have a turn feeding him.

Unbeknownst to Kerri the embassy had gotten a hold of Pastor Ted after they got home that night because he had been handed the Pastor's card and was staying in touch with him so as to keep Kerri from having to feel the yoyo effect of thinking, wandering, and knowing; and Egypt had called Israel, and Israel the US, and supposedly Kerri's parents had been found and was on their way home, but it could still take a few days so the decision was made to wait until they were positive before they told Kerri.

Brad said he would do his best to keep her busy and the guys teased him and told him they knew he was making a sacrifice and they all laughed. So Kerri was ready when Brad came to pick her up the next morning and they were at their first store by five in the morning. They shopped until they dropped and they got good deals on everything and then they went by the tree lot and bought two Christmas trees went to Kerri's first and unloaded and then went to Brad's and unloaded. They went in to eat turkey sandwiches then they found themselves knee deep in decorations and they decorated the tree and his house and it was about four PM when they left to go to her house.

She said, "Brad I'm too tired to decorate tonight..." and she was fast asleep before her last sentence.

Brad didn't want her to see all the activity until he was sure everything had been done and after she went to sleep, he called Pastor Ted and Pastor Ted said the coast was clear.

The Ultimate Gift

Brad was very excited to find everything had went as planned and he felt he had done the right thing by keeping everything from her he didn't want her to be hurt or disappointed. Brad knew he was so in love with her and couldn't imagine his life without her in it now. Brad was still waiting for a word from the Lord just to be absolutely sure. Brad wanted only what God wanted for him and he knew Kerri felt the same but it was getting harder to wait. Brad prayed on the way Lord if we are to be together please let us know if we are not please let us know so we are not walking in the flesh. Lord if you allow me to have this precious angel in my life I promise I will do everything I can to take care of her with your help of course.

Brad got out of the truck and went around to her side of the truck and shook her ever so gently and said alright sweetheart we are at your house you need to get out and stand up beautiful. Kerri heard Brad and smiled but could not open her eyes. Brad had to half carry her to the door he asked where is your key and she said in my bag she fumbled around for it and found it and gave it to Brad and when she walked in the whole house was lit up like a Christmas fairy land and the first thing she saw was her mom and dad standing under a beautifully decorated tree in the middle of fairy land.

Kerri thought she must be dreaming and then she thought that wasn't right if she was dreaming she wouldn't think she was dreaming she was standing in the middle of the floor to figure out what was going on and she said, "You are real, I'm not dreaming am I? You are real." then she threw herself into her mother and dad's arms. "What a wonderful surprise but how? Where? When? Why? Oh I don't care I am so happy. Where have you been? Oh mom, Oh dad, I am so glad you are here."

Kerri was breathless and continued, "I think I am going to faint…" and Brad reached out and caught her.

Pastor Ted had already filled Tom and Deanne in on everything that was going on between Kerri and Brad and who Brad was and how Kerri came and gave her life to the Lord. Kerri looked up at Brad and said Brad it's my mom and dad. Brad grinned and Pastor Ted stepped forward and said, "Tom and Deanne Johnson I would like you to meet Brad Kensington and Brad this Tom and Deanne Johnson Kerri's mom and dad."

Kerri then looked around and saw all of her Christmas decorations had been put up and she was so amazed at how beautiful everything looked but boy did she have some questions. Brad reached out his hand to shake Tom's and Deanne grabbed him and hugged him.

They said, "It is so good to meet you."

"It is wonderful to meet you."

Tom said, "Thank you for everything you did."

Brad replied, "All I did was make a couple of calls."

Kerri was very confused and she said, "I feel like I have entered the twilight zone."

Brad gave her a hug and said, "Tonight I want you to be with your parents and enjoy them to night and then I will get together with you and your parents tomorrow afternoon if that would be okay."

Kerri said, "Sure I will trust you and not ask any questions now but when you come tomorrow you better be ready for a barrage of questions" and then everyone left to leave her alone with her parents.

Tom and Deanne were standing behind Kerri and Tom said, "If you think she is going let you off the hook on all of those questions you have another thing coming so you might as well come on over in the morning because I am not answering all of her questions." He looked at his daughter and said, "I hope you don't mind if I invite someone to your house since you sold mine."

Kerri blushed and turned and said, "As you can see my dad is home."

Brad leaned down and kissed her on the cheek and walked out the door he thought he had never seen her look sweeter like a little girl and he stated laughing and Kerri could hear him all the way to his truck. It was all Tom and Deanne could do not to fall over laughing themselves and they looked at each other and thought, *Our little girl is in love.*

Kerri's dad said, "Okay my little girl, I know you have a thousand questions and we will answer them tomorrow but I have traveled thousands of miles and I don't have the strength right now" and he added, "Where do we sleep?"

Kerri was glad, she had bought the town home with two master bedrooms and her parent's things that she kept were in that room. She led her parents to their room and her mother gasped because it was so beautiful a mixture of old and new and her Dad said, "Look ladies we can talk tomorrow."

Kerri said, "Good night and I love you."

"We love you too kiddo," her dad said good night.

After she had laid down in her bed she thought how had Brad achieved finding and getting her parents when all of Israel and the United States couldn't find them. From what Kerri had gathered by hearing everything that was said it was something Brad had set in action to get things rolling she was very appreciative and she knew she was in love with him but would he want her once he found out about her past.

Help Comes in Unusual Ways

Brad went home and had a cup of hot coco it really was a lot colder and the forecast did call for snow so he kept thinking about coco all the way home. As he was drinking his coco he thought a lot about Kerri how she had grown in the Lord and so fast she seemed she couldn't get enough of the Lord and he felt the Lord had told him tonight as he was on his way home that she was to be his wife but he wanted complete and total confirmation from the Lord.

Sometimes Kerri seemed older than her years and sometimes she seemed like a little girl. Oh there was no doubt he was definitely in love. Brad thought she was beautiful. He knew what he had done by contacting Abdul was risky but he felt as if he had heard from the Lord to reach out to him to see if he could help to find Kerri's parents but at the point the Ambassador said they were in the case he didn't see how it could hurt.

Brad had contacted the Ambassador that evening after he left Kerri's and told him about the friend he had made in college Brad told the Ambassador that everyone was being mean to Abdul because he was a Muslim and Brad could not stand to see anyone bullied for any reason and not only that but he could not for the life of him figure out how anyone could witness to someone if they did not first show the love of Christ. Brad had reached out to Abdul and befriended him and Abdul seemed to have respect for Brad because he had reached out to him.

Brad had talked to Abdul about Jesus many time but so far Abdul still believed that Jesus was just a nice teacher. Brad had prayed for Abdul to become a Christian ever since he met him and Brad stayed in contact with Abdul. Abdul was a young man from a wealthy very well connected family in Egypt. Connected in the way Brad thought might help. When he had spoken with the ambassador that evening, the ambassador said, "I don't want to know any names, so if you do this you do this on your own but I can give you all the information I have and maybe that will be of help"

Brad said, "Thank you sir," and hung up.

After that Brad called Abdul immediately and Abdul stopped him after his first few sentences and said, "I am sorry I cannot help you with such a thing."

Brad said, "Thank you," and hung up thinking, *oh well that was the end of that.* But about two hours later Abdul called him back and said he had to go to a secure line and now they could talk so Brad told Abdul what was going on and Abdul teased him and said, "I see friend you are in love no?" Abdul laughed and Brad asked him was there anyway he could help and Abdul said, "Let me make some calls and I will let you know as soon as I can, but go ahead and give me the information you have and I will see if anything can be done."

"Thank you Abdul" and Brad said "I am still praying for you."

Abdul laughed, "We will not talk of that this time good bye, friend."

Brad hung up and prayed for Abdul first to find Christ and then for him to be able to succeed in getting help for Kerri's parents. Brad had almost given up hope of Abdul being able to do anything to help in the situation about a week before thanksgiving he received a call from Abdul and he said everything was ago but that is all he would say. Brad called Ambassador Levine and the Ambassador said he had just received a call from his contacts and they said that the Johnson's would be put on a plane to America as soon as possible. And that was the last he had heard until right before Thanksgiving and he didn't know they would be here this soon but he decided to keep Kerri busy as he could and then get some help to give her a real surprise and it seemed everything went off without a hitch, that is if she wasn't mad at him for keeping her in the dark.

He still didn't know everything about how Abdul had found them or where they had been or anything he was just happy they were ok and made it home. Brad knew at some point Tom would sit down with him and tell him everything he knew at least he may never know about Abdul's end but that was ok with him. Brad was going to have to turn the prayers up on Abdul and he knew just who to get to help him pray. At least Tom and Deanne didn't look as if they had been hurt in anyway and Brad wondered where had they been then he thought that thought will have to wait for morning.

Brad was glad everything turned out as well as it did; about the time he was about to drift off, Ambassador Levine called and said, "Young man I do not know what kind of contacts you have but I know who to call in case of a crises." Brad said, "No sir this was a one time endeavor and the Ambassador said he was glad everything worked out the way it had." Brad told him good night and hung up and fell into a very restful sleep.

Getting Out of Egypt

Kerri slept like a log she hadn't slept that well since before her parents disappearance she usually awoke at least one time during the night but last night she slept all night until she smelled coffee bacon and biscuits and when she opened her eyes her mother was standing over her and said, "Come on honey, it is ten o'clock and I have missed my little girl."

Kerry bounded out of bed and into her mother's arms and, "Oh mom I've missed you and daddy so much I am so glad you are home." Kerri heard a big booming voice coming from the other room and said, "I'm glad to be home too" and she ran and jumped into her father's arms.

Kerri's dad said, "Okay honey go get dressed, I went and did some shopping this morning, so I could have a big breakfast and I don't want it held up."

Kerri said, "Okay Daddy I'll go and get ready."

Kerri took the fastest shower in history she didn't want to waste a second. Kerri felt someone ought to start telling her something pretty soon She didn't ask that many questions last night because she knew they were only operating on raw energy but she wanted to know what had happened and the how, when, and where of it all. When she walked into the kitchen she heard her father on the phone and he was saying, "Come on over and then we will talk" and hung up and turned and saw the disappointed look on her face and he said, "If I know you and I know you probably haven't changed that much. You were on your way in here to start firing questions like a machine gun and I don't mind answering them but I want to have this talk once, and then be done with it and I feel since Brad is the main reason we are standing here then he ought to be included in the conversation."

Kerri grinned from ear to ear and said, "Daddy you do still know me."

Tom added, "Besides I am not sure of everything that happened myself, so with Brad here maybe he can help us to understand what did happen."

Kerri said, "Okay dad but can we eat I am starved." Then she poured orange juice and coffee for everyone and they sat down and ate breakfast.

Brad showed up after they had everything put away he came in and said, "It is really good to see you Mr. and Mrs. Johnson"

"It's good to see you too but please call us Tom and Deanne, Brad."

So he sat down and had a cup of coffee and Kerri asked him if he wanted any breakfast and he said no but he was making her wait a little but he could tell she was getting impatient.

Finally she said, "That's it Brad, mom, and dad I want answers and I want them now.

Brad looked at Tom and Deanne and asked is she always this pushy and then she looked as if she was about to explode and Tom said, "Okay before you see how big of a fit she can throw, let's move to the living room and get started."

Kerri shrugged her shoulders and threw her head back and Brad started laughing until she gave him the look. Tom said, "Well mom she's still got it"

Deanne replied, "Yes she does."

Brad asked, "What?"

Tom said, "Why looks that can kill in more ways than one my dear boy."

Brad whispered to Tom where Kerri couldn't hear and he said, "I think I have already been wounded by one."

Tom said, "I believe you have dear boy; I believe you have."

By that time everyone was settled in the living room with a fresh cup of coffee. Brad said, "Why don't you start at the beginning Tom."

Tom said, "Well it was our last two weeks of the trip and we wanted to get home before the end of September, so we could do things that needed to be done before fall and all the festivities started but we really wanted to see how the Israelites left Egypt and wilderness experience but in order to get that tour you had to go to Egypt so we finally got all of our papers in order and we took like a commuter plane to Egypt.

"The trouble started on the first leg of our journey at first everything seemed fine and the flight attendant came on and said we would be landing in Egypt on time and gave the time and how we would be flying over and described what we were flying over. Then about twenty or thirty minutes into the flight, the flight attendant came on and said we would be making an emergency landing well needless to say that made our hair stand on end. We landed without incident the flight attendant came ask us just to relax they would have some one here to pick us up and take us to the nearest airport well we sat there for a while and nothing seemed to be happening.

"Deanne and I lookout of the plane's window. There was nothing but desert, and we just didn't see anything we could do, so we prayed and ask the Lord for help. The flight attendant had disappeared and was the only one that spoke any English and he didn't seem to want to talk with us anymore, but shortly there after he came and escorted several people off the plane that seemed to know exactly what they were doing. There were only five other people on the plane and looked as frightened as we felt, Deanne and I both knew we could be in for some trouble so we decided to just put our trust in the Lord.

"I decided to get up and go see what was going on up front and I couldn't find any of the people who had gotten off the plane. The flight attendant had disappeared and I spoke to one of the five people on the plane who spoke a little broken English, but he kept saying something about spies and that we were at an old abandoned military base at least as far as I could understand. Then all of the sudden one of the passengers answered his phone and he said something to the other four, and they got up and left so we decided to follow them and as they were starting to get off the plane through the emergency chute there was a bus pull up and the five got on, but would not let us on kept saying something about spies and left us there.

"All that was there was a few old broken down buildings and a couple of hangers, By this time I knew it would be getting dark and cold in a little while so we had to figure out what we needed to do so we prayed and ask the Holy Spirit to give us ideas. Well we didn't want to spend the night outside especially in a country we knew nothing about and the buildings didn't look much better, so I went looking for things we could use and then in one of the old hangers I found one of those stairs on wheels that you put up to a plane to get on and off the ones they used years ago and I looked at it and the wheels still looked good.

"So I pushed it and found it rolled just fine and so we pushed it up to the planes door they had left that door open thank God and we were able to get back in the plane it was loaded with food and pillows and blankets so we fixed ourselves something to eat and took all the pillows and blankets and made beds for ourselves because we didn't know what else to do we figured the Lord had a plan so we went to sleep and when we awoke the next morning and had a breakfast of fresh fruit peanut butter crackers water and juice. I tried we tried our cell phones and even the radio on the plane and couldn't get anything to work. Deanne looked at me and said, 'Well we wanted the wilderness experience,' and we both laughed we were totally dependant on the Lord we had provisions for a few days and we were to where the animals could get to us so we felt we had to wait on the Lords guidance and so we waited.

"We even got out of the plane during the day and walked around the old military base. We found a lot of provisions in a shed and the dates on them were still good; there was water and packages of military meals was as if they were expecting someone to stay there, and we were there for a while we lost track of time, and we were beginning to think when these ran out we might die.

"One day this van pulls up out of no where and orders us in and we get in and then they took us to this small village like place and there were these adobe like sheds and they put each of us in one and questioned us for two days apart and two days together they kept saying we were spies and we were very confused even though we were still trusting God and we both had perfect peace. We were allowed to shower and given our clothes that had been stashed on the plane and very well cared for we just didn't know why they kept calling us spies. We were never abused in anyway we still till this day do not know why all of it happened or why we were called spies."

Brad then spoke up and said, "I think I have that part." Brad continued, "The plane you got on was the wrong one and they didn't know each other, so they thought you were a part of them but when they real-ized you weren't with them they thought you might be from the other side and you were planted spies it was part of planning a coupe and they were all going there together well when they realized you weren't with them they had to do something drastic so they landed at that old military base and left you thinking you might find you way out or die but then they decided to come find you to make sure you didn't put a kink in their plans.

"They didn't know for sure what to do with you so they decided to take care of you until they could decide. Brad said it is only by the race of God you weren't killed because they had just about decided to do away with you when Abdul got involved, you see no one even knew about you other than the Israeli Embassy and the United States, so they did not know where you came from.

"Abdul had to be very careful because it was a very sensitive situation and he did not want it to become political any more than Israel did oh by the way your things from your hotel in Israel are being sent to you and Ambassador Levine says shalom and he hopes this won't keep you from visiting his country. They both said they would go to Israel tomorrow just not any other country right now."

Kerri said, "I hope you aren't going anywhere any-way soon."

They both said they thought they need some rest. Kerri jumped up and gave Brad a big hug and kissed him and said, "Thank you for bringing my parents home."

Brad said, "If he knew it would cause that kind of stir, he would have rushed it up."

Then Kerri's dad asked her if he and her mother were declared legally dead and she said no they had to be missing longer. Tom asked her, "Well, how did you sell the house?"

"You gave me power of attorney remember?

"Oh, that's right."

"I am sorry about the house."

They both said they thought she did fine they liked this house and they were planning to downsize and her dad said, "You will marry and leave us one day anyway."

Kerri blushed all the way to her toes and looked up. Brad was smiling down at her and was thinking, *There's that little girl again.*

Brad said, "Wear something really warm, and I will be back around five to pick you up. I am going to take everyone to dinner, the Christmas parade, and Christmas tree lighting, unless you guys are too tired." No one objected; they were all looking forward to it.

Kerri's Secret

Kerri and Deanne decided to go and do some shopping after Brad left because her mom and Dad needed something warm to wear that night and it had been a long time since they had had any mom and daughter time together and her dad wanted to look the house over and the basement while they were gone he would be in his element looking the house over and seeing what he might want to add he and her mom both said they were very happy about the house and would have selected the same one if it had been them looking.

Deanne asked Kerri if she had gotten rid of her life size Nativity Sean and Kerri said, "No mom, I would never do something like that I love that Nativity Sean as much as you do" and she told her mom that the only reason it wasn't out is because she hadn't had time to put it out and she said, "Besides we used to put it out the Sunday after Thanksgiving so lets do it tomorrow after church okay?"

Her mom said that that sounded lovely. "Kerri?" Deanne said

"Yes, mom"

Her mom cleared her throat and asked her, "How serious are you about this young man?

Kerri turned to her mom and said, "I am praying about that and so is he."

Deanne smiled and said, "It is so good to hear you talk like that. I know you walked the isle when you were a child, but I am so glad to know you have given your whole life to the Lord and see you truly walking with him and in him. It shows all over you and I believe if I am not mistaken you are in love with Brad but have you…"

Kerri said, "Not yet mom, but I am going to tell him tonight."

"Okay honey, you don't won't to ever have anything hidden from someone you care about."

"I know mom, I did tell him about your and dad's story and he thought it was a precious story, so maybe he can handle this."

Deanne said, "Okay honey, your dad and I will be praying."

Kerri and her mom had a wonderful day of shopping and even had a manicure and a pedicure and went home and rested then got dressed her mom and dad in there new warm up suits. Brad picked them up at five and they went for and early dinner at the steak house he had taken her to the Sunday after she gave her life to the Lord.

So by the time the parade and Christmas tree lighting was over Tom and Deanne were ready for a good night sleep so they would be ready for church the next day and they knew they would be bombarded by their friends. Kerri told Brad after he had taken them home that her mom had mentioned the Nativity Sean and Kerri said she wished she had gotten around to getting it out and Brad said, "Well, if your not too tired, how about now?"

She said, "Really?"

He said that, "The guys put the outside lights up the other day but we didn't want to draw your attention to your house. so they didn't turn them on."

So after they had set up the Nativity Sean and were getting ready to go in and drink some hot coco Kerri told Brad there was something she needed to tell him and he looked at her and said okay and she said, "Well this not easy and I should never have waited this long to tell you and you may never want to see me again after I tell you this, but my mother told me today that I needed to be honest and tell you everything and keep nothing hidden."

By this time Brad was more than a little alarmed and he said, "Kerri you can tell me anything, please go ahead."

Kerri started shaking from nerves and was tearing up and then Brad said, "Kerri what is it you are scaring me."

Kerri said, "Brad when I was young I had one summer I was very wild I got on drugs I was rebellious and I gave my mom and dad some real trouble. I was hooked on drugs and I wanted to try everything. I was totally out of control. My mom and dad was trying very hard to help me but I didn't want their help or anyone else's.

I thought I knew better all this happened during summer break, so thank goodness my grades didn't suffer.

"I don't really know why but all I wanted was the next high I was looking for excitement I just wanted to feel good. Thank God I was never raped and didn't get into sex for drugs but only by the grace of God as I look back on it now. If my mom and dad hadn't done an intervention and got me in rehab I would probably be on the street corner or dead by now anyway I was always in possession of one kind of a drug or another so I wouldn't let them help me until one night a guy followed me home and my dad got beat up trying to protect me and the next day they did the intervention and I went to a rehab center.

"Anyway, there is always a chance of an addict slipping up, but I have been clean for a long time now."

Kerri suddenly stopped and looked up at Brad and said, "So if you never want to see me again it will be okay."

She really started crying and Brad grabbed her so quickly and held her so tight he was afraid he might break her and he said, "Kerri there is not one thing that you could tell me that would make me not want you. Kerri the Word says 'For all have sinned and come short of the Glory of God.' Romans 3:23 Do you know what Jesus said to scribes and Pharisees when the adulterous woman who was caught in adultery? Jesus said 'He that is without sin among you, let him cast the first stone at her,' John 8:7 Kerri I am not good enough and you are not good enough; no one is. What you call good enough that is the reason God sent his Son to die on the cross that we might live and have eternal life.

"'But we are all as an unclean thing, and all our right-eousness are as filthy rags; and we all do fade as a leaf; and our inequities, like the wind have taken us away.' Isaiah 64:6 'For God so loved the world that he gave His only begotten Son that whosoever would believe in Him would not perish but have ever lasting life.' John 3:16 It is only through the Lord that we can love anyone and 1 Corinthians 13 says, 'Now abide faith, hope, and love but the greatest of these is love.'

'Kerri, I can't love you without Christ, I can lust, I can possess, but true and real love only come from the Father our creator, you see love is wanting the absolute best for another person without selfishness, or manipulation just wanting the best for them. Kerri wasn't planning on telling you this yet but I can't put it off any longer I planned to wait just a little longer but I love you Kerri I want us to be together all the time I am hoping you love me too."

Kerri was crying happy tears and she said, "Yes, Brad I love you too."

"Will you marry me Kerri and they kissed until Brad pulled back and said now when are we getting married."

The Beginning

As Brad and Kerri stood in front of Pastor Ted and said their vows on Christmas Eve afternoon. Kerri and Brad decided to get married in a chapel on a hill that had an open glass view floor to ceiling overlooking Christmas Town. The decorations were sparkling and making the snow even more festive. It was a beautiful wedding and Kerri had no trouble finding the perfect white wedding dress it fit perfectly with a tight bodice and a v neck slightly off the shoulders, and a v fitted waist line with the softest gauziest material, tiny pearl buttons down the back with the sleeves coming to a v over the backs of her hands.

Kerri' long dark curly hair was pulled up and slightly back and caught up in a diamond like tiara and let fall down her back what a beautiful picture she made. Brad was in a black tux and looked very handsome and dashing. They had a small beautiful wedding just what they both wanted but the main persons in the wedding was the Father, Son , and The Holy Spirit the Holy Spirit was very strong and there was such peace, love, and joy. That is who David and Kerri are Two people who love Jesus Christ first and each other second. They turned and Pastor Ted said, "May I present Mr. and Mrs. Bradford Preston Kensington."

Everyone rose and clapped. Kerri and Brad took off for their honey moon that evening and went up into the mountains where Brad had a cabin stocked with everything from wood to gourmet food so they would have everything they need for a few days. They had a wonderful honeymoon. About four months later Kerri called Brad after her doctor's appointment on Friday afternoon and suggested a night out on the town. Brad took her to a beautiful restaurant overlooking the river and close to the chapel they had gotten married in and the first touches of spring was in the air. After dinner they took a stroll down town and they passed by some shops that were open and told brad she wanted to go in and look at something.

Brad said, "Alright, I will stay right here if you will hurry back"

She smiled at her wonderful husband realizing how blessed she really was. As soon as Kerri returned she handed Brad a beautifully wrapped gift and he said what is this and she said, "Something that just caught my eye."

Brad opened the box and in it lay an infant sleeper and on the front it said, "I'm my daddy's baby." Brad stood staring at the article for a minute and then he let out a holler and hugged and kissed her and said, "It's Springtime in Christmas Town."

"Yes, it's always springtime in Christmas town darling, always springtime in Christmas town." Kerri agreed.

Lightning Source UK Ltd.
Milton Keynes UK
UKOW07f1935141214

243121UK00013B/161/P

9 781629 942841